MORE PRAISE FO

"Every small town h[...]el introduces us to th[...]hind the cheery facad[...] for how real people sp[...], and a wisdom about how real people do and don't solve their problems, Thornton's riveting debut earns its place on the shelf of contemporary Southern classics."
—WILTON BARNHARDT, author of *Lookaway, Lookaway*

"In *Lord the One You Love is Sick*, Kasey Thornton, with a clear eye and a kind heart, expertly navigates the currents in the small pond that is the contemporary Southern town of Bethany, North Carolina. Her broad cast of well-realized characters demonstrate how the everyday assumptions in such a town can consign people to neglect and misunderstanding, and how individuals struggle against those internalized definitions to create their own lives. A cry for charity."
—JOHN KESSEL, author of *Pride and Prometheus*

"What a pleasure it was to discover a book like this, at this moment, when the cultural conversation is running always towards opinion. Here is the realm of fiction, with its love of failure and difficulty, it's respect for broken humanity. This intelligent, young writer is alive with talent, and these serious, beautiful, funny stories should be read carefully."—REBECCA LEE, author of *Bobcat and Other Stories*

"Propulsive, painful, sharp-edged and shot through with redemption, Kasey Thornton's *Lord the One You Love is Sick* belongs on a shelf with Bobbie Ann Mason's *Shiloh* and Sherwood Anderson's *Winesburg, Ohio*. Read it not just for the deep satisfaction of seeing the plot quilt itself together: read it because

these people are family, because they're the people we fear we could be, and because, ultimately, they're the people we hope we might become. The ending comes at you like a train in the night. I could not put it down. Lord, I loved this book."
—DREW PERRY, author, *This Is Exactly Like You*

Lord the One
You Love Is Sick

Lord the One
You Love Is Sick

a novel in stories

KASEY THORNTON

New York, NY

Printed in the United States of America
10 9 8 7 6 5 4 3 2 1

No part of this book may be used or reproduced in any manner
without written permission of the publisher. Please direct inquires
to:

Ig Publishing
Box 2547
New York, NY 10163
www.igpub.com

ISBN: 978-1-63246-117-9 (paperback)

For Mama, Kevin, Mandy, and Sherlock

A man named Lazarus was ill. He lived in the village of Bethany with his sisters, Mary and Martha. The sisters sent a message to Jesus: "Lord, the one you love is sick."

Jesus heard it and said, "This sickness is for God's glory," and though he loved Martha, Mary, and Lazarus, he stayed where he was for two more days.

When it was time to leave, his disciples questioned him. Jesus said, "Lazarus is dead. For your sake, I am glad I was not there to save him, so that you may believe."

When Jesus arrived in Bethany, he found that Lazarus had indeed been dead for four days. Martha met him outside. "Lord, if you'd been here, my brother would not have died."

Jesus said to her, "Your brother will rise again."

The other sister Mary knelt at Jesus' feet, weeping. "Lord, if you'd been here, my brother would not have died."

The Jews whispered, "Could he not have kept this man from dying?"

Jesus said to Mary and Martha, "Did I not tell you that if you believed, you would see the glory of God? Take away the stone."

—John 11

What is said, what is left to the imagination, what is denied, withheld, exaggerated—all these secretive, inverted things informed my childhood . . . I remember being particularly fascinated by secrets kept in order to protect someone from who you are. That protection, sharpest knife in the drawer, I absorbed as naturally as a Southern accent.

—Frances Mayes,
Under Magnolia: A Southern Memoir

CONTENTS

I SHALL NOT WANT

THE TASER FELT LIKE NAIL GUNS FIRING into him from all directions. His legs locked up like stone pillars inside of his regulation khakis, keeping him on his feet, as he hoped they would. For the last hour, he'd listened to the electric *clickclickclickclick* as the trainees took their turns being tased by the instructors, but when those prongs activated on him, he could only barely make out the sound as he clenched his teeth and bobbed his head.

When it stopped, his entire body relaxed with a whoosh. His muscles were sore, but the bite of the shock was gone instantly.

"It's so much better than being pepper-sprayed," Griggs said, to whoever was listening, for the tenth time. He was next in line after Dale. "When you're tased, it's over when it's over, you know? Doesn't linger."

They unclipped the prongs from Dale's shirt, and he lifted his sleeve to examine the small, bruise-like burns they left behind.

Griggs was a few years older than Dale, maybe late twenties. He handed his cell phone to the trainee behind him, still mumbling anxiously, "Tased is better. When you're sprayed, it's never over. Not for a long time." The instructors took a pinch of his navy polo and clipped the prongs on his arm. "Tased is much better than getting sprayed."

Dale wasn't sure why Griggs was trying to comfort himself with the thought of being pepper-sprayed. They'd all be pepper-sprayed that afternoon. It was rough, but most of them were happy to get it all over with at one time. One uncomfortable day, one uncomfortable night, and then they'd all move on.

It was an unseasonably cool morning, the first truly chilly day of the season. For Dale, autumn only meant less sweating and more comfortable clothes, but it was an extended holiday of its own around here. The bakery in Bethany was decorated with fake spider-webs and long-nosed stuffed witches and pumpkin-spice muffins on glass cake holders. His girlfriend Charlotte,, who everyone called Charlie, had already decked out their front porch with hay bales from Nettie Coats' farm and half-rotten pumpkins from a pallet in front of the grocery store. "Those'll never last until Halloween," he had told her.

"Well, they're not *Halloween* pumpkins," she said. "Halloween pumpkins have faces on them, dummy." She was happy to finally have a place of their own, one that she could clean and fancy up and burn down if she wanted to, so he gave her free reign where the décor was concerned. He didn't care much.

From here, Dale could catch the moldy smell of the community college pond down the hill that they jogged around three times a week for PT. Last week they arrived at sunrise and discovered that someone had dumped way too much turquoise dye into it over the weekend in preparation for campus visits. Graduating seniors from Bethany High School without the money to go anywhere else ended up here, all saying the same thing—"I'll get my basic classes out of the way where it's cheap and then transfer"—before dropping out after a semester or two.

Dale's best friend Gentry did this, or that's what he heard. It was a small town, and he didn't want it getting to Sergeant Simmons of the Bethany Police Department that he hung out with someone who had a laundry-list of misdemeanor drug offenses. Dale was in training on a scholarship that paid for his books, uniform, and tuition, and Simmons had hinted more than once that he was trying to find a place for him after he graduated.

After lunch, the trainees went around to the back of the building near the dumpsters and stood in a line again.

"It stinks back here," someone said.

"You won't be able to smell anything in a minute."

An instructor wearing a mask aimed a can of pepper spray at Dale's forehead, point-blank, and pulled the trigger. There was a full minute of "oh my God" and "holy shit" and "fuck, fuck, fuck, fuck" and teeth-gritting before they had to take turns wrestling one another into handcuffs. It felt like two halves of a fresh onion soaked in ghost-pepper juice had been rubbed onto Dale's eyes. They watered uncontrollably onto the front of his shirt, making it impossible to see anything.

By the end of the day, Dale had been tased, tear-gassed, and pepper-sprayed, all in the name of justice, all in the name of "knowing how it feels." He stood on the curb out front, waiting for Charlie with snot coming from seemingly every hole in his face.

He knew he was facing a conniption whenever she arrived to see him like this. Charlie didn't need to *say* she had issues with him going into law enforcement, but it was obvious every time he came home sore from PT, every time he studied his textbook at the dinner table. He knew her reasons were the same as every other woman whose man wore a uniform, and he couldn't fault her for it. Maybe he was supposed to, but he didn't.

Dale heard a truck approaching and knew it was Charlie by the grinding sound it made when she stopped in front of him. The passenger door was shoved open in his direction.

"You need to go to Earl's and get brake pads on this thing," he said, pulling himself inside and groping blindly for the seatbelt.

"Ten bucks if you go home and do it for me this afternoon," she said.

"I don't want to deny Jackson the pleasure."

Charlie laughed, then fell uncharacteristically quiet. Usually she launched into the daily report on her endearingly alcoholic father and self-righteous mother, or something on the news she knew he'd missed by being in class all day, or whatever else came to her mind. She was chatty and opinionated and he wasn't either of those things, but he liked the sound of her voice.

Today was different. They had to drive all the way down Thigpen Road, which crossed through three different towns in the county, and she said maybe ten words the entire time. He filled the space by telling her about the onion-peppers in his eyes and the prong bruises on his arm, punctuated with a few fun tidbits about lethal injections he'd learned in class. At some point, she muttered that she had some chicken breasts in the slow-cooker for dinner.

As soon as they got home, she helped him out of his shirt and bent him backward over the kitchen sink to wash the remnants of the spray out of his hair so he could shower without it dripping back down onto his face. He cautiously cracked open one eye to see that her mouth was puckered, her face contorted in a pre-cry wince.

"Did you call me today while I was in class?"

"Yeah. I'm sorry."

"What is it?"

"Gentry's dead."

Dale tried to stand up, but she pushed him down.

"Don't," she said. "It'll get all over your face."

Dale remembered Gentry standing on the back of his parents' farmhouse last summer, smoking a menthol. Dale remembered Gentry offering him a Coors, which he refused for the first time in a decade. Dale remembered Gentry's bitter laugh when Dale told him that if he didn't get his shit straight, they wouldn't be seeing as much of each other. "I'm going into law enforcement, man," Dale had said. "I'm going into law enforcement and your ass can't stop getting in trouble. How's that going to look? Have you thought about that?" Dale remembered squinting to figure out if the black and blue tint on the inside of Gentry's elbow was a trick of the porch light. He remembered seeing the red punctures. He remembered the way Gentry flicked his cigarette in the grass—so final—the way he said, "Do what you want, man. Fuck it."

He said that a lot. *Fuck it.*

Dale didn't need to ask Charlie how he died. "Who found him?"

"Let me get the top, Dale."

"Who found him?"

"Ethan."

"Christ." Gentry's younger brother was Charlie's age. Thinking about him made Dale think about Gentry's father, and thinking about his father made him think about Gentry's mother. He thought about what it'd be like to face Nettie Coats after this.

"It looks like Tang," Charlie said to the chemicals in the sink, her voice shaking. "It looks like orange juice. Does it hurt?"

"It will for a while," he answered.

The doorway of the Coats' farmhouse was marked with one of those white oval wreaths in case someone didn't know, or couldn't tell by all the cars in the yard. When Dale and Charlie arrived, they saw Nettie standing in the living room, wearing blue jeans and the nicest black blouse she owned, with tiny silver sequins along the collar. It was a western shirt, a Dolly Parton shirt. Her face was an angry, swollen red. Dale tried to make eye contact with her from across the room, to gauge her reaction to his presence, but she avoided looking at him. Dale wondered what she knew.

Ethan was a chubby little guy who had the perpetual look of someone who wanted to slam the pause button and reset to his last save point. He was standing awkwardly in the kitchen between his father, Earl, and Earl's business partner, Jackson Hatcher. Jackson worked at the garage that Earl owned on Third Street.

When Dale and Charlie finished laying their coats over a chair in the foyer, Jackson pointed at the two of them with his finger, smiling and pushing through the crowd. "Goddamn it," Charlie hissed, taking Dale's arm in both hands as though to pull herself into his protection. "I can't stand that man. He gives me the creeps."

"Crazy Hatcher?" Dale whispered. "He's harmless. The sixties just weren't kind to him."

"Hey boy," Jackson said too loud, extending his hand and ignoring Charlie completely. "Kind of trouble you into these days?"

"Training," Dale said. "Law enforcement."

"Ought've seen that coming. Simmons know you looking

for a job?"

"He's the one that got me the scholarship. I'll be on in Bethany by Thanksgiving."

"Shit," Hatcher said, with two syllables. "You'll get yourself killed out there, man, the way niggers is raising hell these days, shooting cops all over the place."

"I don't think we need to worry about that," Charlie blurted, not bothering to hide her fist-clenching irritation with him.

Jackson ignored her. "They training you on Smith & Wessons?"

"Glocks."

"Hell," Hatcher snorted, and Charlie took a step back as though he planned to spit right on her toe. "Can't beat the feel of a Smith in your hand," he said reverently, as if he were quoting the Bible. "Know what I mean?"

"I know what you mean," Dale said.

"I'm teaching my youngest on a Beretta 92."

"Your youngest *daughter*?"

"Damn skippy."

"Well, I'm going to see Nettie," Charlie said, pinching Dale's arm.

"I'll come with you. Take it easy, man."

"*You* take it easy on *me*, boy. Simmons always did," Hatcher said, pushing open the screen door and disappearing onto the back porch for a smoke.

Nettie was suddenly beside them, as though she'd been waiting the whole time for Jackson to leave. "Simmons took it easy on Gentry, too," she said. "We see how that turned out."

Charlie turned and wrapped Nettie in her arms. They stuck their foreheads into one another's shoulders the way women do. She'd always had a soft spot for Charlie. "I hate these goddamn church people," Nettie whispered, her shoulders shaking a little bit. "Didn't do shit for us when he was alive except tell him he couldn't come to church socials and now they're gonna throw themselves at me? I won't have it."

"You shouldn't have it," Charlie said, pulling back. "We didn't know he was so bad."

"Obviously not," she said, looking at Dale. "I'm sure you would've done something to help."

"Yes ma'am," Dale said.

"Other than leave him to die on the floor in his own shit?"

Dale's face got hot.

Charlie said, "How's Ethan?"

"Fat," Nettie said. "Weird. Playing video games non-stop."

"Like an escape, maybe?"

"I reckon. He broke up with that girlfriend of his. His *current* one."

Charlie rolled her eyes. She and Ethan had dated briefly in middle school and Nettie liked to tease them about it. "You're talking about Mary Stuart?"

"Yup. Funeral home came by to get Gentry out of here, and Ethan got on the phone with her as soon as they left. She didn't seem to do much for him, anyway. I ain't found a single condom."

"*Nettie*," Charlie hissed and shoved her. "You better hush."

"Oh, it's my own damn house," Nettie said loudly, then looked over at Ethan as he fumbled with a casserole dish in the kitchen. "I don't know if there's anyone out there who can do anything for him. He's gotten so timid and quiet since."

"Maybe not for a while," Dale said. He didn't *want* to talk to her, but he also didn't want her to think he was deliberately avoiding it.

"You coming to the funeral?" she asked him.

"Of course," Dale said.

"Well, I'd like for you to sit with the family," Nettie said, like she was offering him a wonderful, poisoned steak out of the goodness of her heart.

"I really don't think that's appropriate."

"No, I think it's appropriate that you have a front-row seat. You were his best friend."

On the way home, Charlie kept the radio off. This was something she did when she knew Dale had a lot on his mind, cutting off different stimulations—the lights, the television, the phones, the noise. He never asked her to do it, but it was one of the things he appreciated about her, one of the things he'd thank her for, if he knew the words to do it with.

"She was in a *mood*," Charlie said.

"She thinks I kicked Gentry to the curb because I want to be a cop and can't associate with users like that."

"To be fair, that's exactly what you did," Charlie said.

"I know."

Dale watched the white line on the side of the road and tried to conjure up any memory of Gentry from high school, from before. He could form mental images of the hallways and the grassy area, the trees by the cafeteria, the taste of bad pizza and red Gatorade, the smell of the compost buckets behind the horticulture greenhouses where he and Charlie snuck off and kissed for the first time. He could see the students bumping shoulders at the big intersections in the stairwells. His mind landed in the umpire box by the baseball field where he and Gentry would smoke cigarettes after school, flicking tiny yellow pencils back and forth to one another and chipping the white paint from the walls.

But when Dale thought of the umpire box, he was alone in it. When he pictured the concrete pad outside of the wood-shop, he was alone. When he thought about the tailgate of Gentry's Dodge, Dale was the only one sitting on it.

He panicked when he realized that his mind had erased all evidence that the pre-addiction Gentry had ever existed.

"I can't," he said suddenly. His voice sounded far away from himself.

"Can't what?" Charlie said.

"I gotta stop."

"Well stop, then."

He pulled into the makeshift dirt lot on the other side of Coolie's Dam where people parked when they wanted to fish off the bridge. He imagined himself sitting here, in this parking lot, in one of the black police Dodge Chargers, catching people going forty-eight, and writing tickets for expired registrations, and not saving Gentry in time for the rest of his life.

As his breathing got ragged, Charlie took off her seatbelt, threw back the center console, and moved toward him on the seat. She pulled his head against her breasts and leaned backward, taking him with her, until her shoulders hit the passenger door.

She was the only person he felt comfortable crying in front of, especially now. She didn't coo or fuss; it felt like she was hiding him, giving him a private space.

"Your hair smells like pepper," she said quietly.

Something about the celestial order of things in Bethany was thrown off. Dale felt it hanging over the town like a full moon or an eclipse when he woke up the next morning. He'd been getting up too early lately, but that wasn't unusual. For the last year or so, he'd go several weeks where all he wanted to do was sleep— he'd pass out after dinner and then sleep well into the afternoon if Charlie let him— and then long stretches where he couldn't sleep at all without tossing and turning for a good part of the night. During these times, he still functioned perfectly fine on three or four hours sleep.

Today was one of those days. He didn't want to lay in bed with his thoughts waiting for Charlie to wake up, so he decided to surprise her with breakfast from Austin's. It was a little lunch joint in the same building as the florists' and the bakery, sandwiched between them; it had a painted logo in seventies-style cursive on the front window, eroding a little more each year beneath the tiny fingernails of bored children. Just about the entire town crunched into the tiny space every morning at seven-thirty and every afternoon at twelve-fifteen, fire-code be damned. At these times it was barely big enough for a line to form against the wall. Dale had spent many Saturday mornings as a child eating biscuits on the curb out front, putting his chin on the counter to watch his grilled cheese being made in the foil-lined iron, sneaking into the back room with Gentry to see where the napkins and plastic silverware and styrofoam cups were hidden in boxes so giant that they could both fit in a single one of them. He and Gentry, together in a box.

Folks in Bethany didn't die of heroin overdoses; they died of car accidents and tractor accidents and heart attacks. The occasional death from cancer was especially harrowing in its slow, impending march to the end—the occasional bumps of hope with new treatments and "good days" and surgeries and tricky remissions. But cancer, at least, was not unheard of. A heroin overdose wasn't just an unseemly way to die. It was downright unnatural.

Always mutinous, Nettie had written Gentry's obituary herself (obviously), and she was uncomfortably honest. *He died of an overdose at the age of twenty-three at his home.*

When Dale walked in, the grumbling old men at the large round table at the front of the diner were leaned forward over their newspapers, talking in hushed breaths, slurping their coffee. Usually they growled like fat old hounds about the stock market, what the president was or wasn't doing, and goings-on in places they couldn't point out on a map even if they wanted to.

Sammy Cotter nodded to Dale, who nodded back. The girls behind the counter were pulling on their hairnets and yawning. Austin himself was getting up there in years but had never, to Dale's knowledge, missed a day opening the diner.

"What say, man?" Austin asked.

"Came by to get Charlie some breakfast."

"Sausage biscuit, orange juice?"

"That's it."

"All I got is pulp this morning."

"She'll get over it. Grilled cheese and fries for me."

Austin turned around and threw a sausage onto the long griddle and a grilled cheese into the iron as Dale pulled a five from his wallet.

"I'm real sorry about that Coats boy," Austin said.

Dale handed the five over and tapped the tip cup. Austin threw the change into it and slammed the register closed.

"I think people make decisions," Dale said, suddenly self-righteous. "And at some point you reap from it."

Austin leaned on the counter. "They ought to have gotten some help for that kid. That's why they have places to go, and groups and shit."

Dale reached over and grabbed a lid for Charlie's orange juice as the bells on the door jangled.

"Dale Overton," Tommy Hawthorne said, by way of a greeting.

"Hey, Tommy."

"Did I see in the paper that Gentry Coats died?"

"That's right," Austin said. "Died on Wednesday."

It was too early for this. He and Tommy Hawthorne had gotten along fine in grade school, back when the kid still had acne and braces and peach-fuzz on his upper lip. Once he learned about Skoal and Nickelback he became unbearable, with an attitude to match his teeth. Dale could feel his own insides rattling, a current of agitation buzzing from the center of his chest and out into his limbs.

"Well shit," Tommy said. "Never did expect him to last long, but I am sorry for his Mama."

Austin pulled the grilled cheese out of the iron and wrapped it in paper, tossing it down the counter at Dale who stopped it with his hand. "I heard that," Austin said. "Woman's as fragile as a coal truck, but God never meant for no mother to bury her own child."

Tommy leaned his arms onto the counter. "What'd he die of?"

Dale didn't want to tell him. He didn't want Tommy Hawthorne, or anyone else, to know how Gentry died. He wanted to say that Gentry had died saving a drowning kid, or defending his country in the Middle East, or in a car accident, or in a tragic cooking mishap. Literally anything else.

"Overdose, wasn't it?" Austin said.

"Well, he died of stupidity, then," Tommy said.

Dale closed his eyes, enraged. He tried to focus on the sizzle of the grill and the scrape of Austin's spatula on it. He breathed along to the rhythm of a commercial jingle on the one television hanging on the wall for ballgames. He dug crescent moons into his palms and opened his eyes to see Tommy smirking like he himself hadn't been all over the front of the *Slammer* two years ago for a DUI.

"He never was right in the head, was he?" Tommy said, to no one in particular.

Shithead needs to shut the fuck up, a voice in Dale's head murmured. *Make him shut up, man.*

Dale grabbed the paper bag of food roughly when Austin passed it to him.

"Thanks Austin, take care Tommy."

"Take care of yourself, Dale."

He pushed through the front door, bells jangling to announce his exit. He threw the bag into the front seat of his truck, opened his glove compartment, and stared at the thick black handle of his Glock.

He needed to chill. He needed to count to ten.

The problem wasn't that you didn't know. You knew. It was that you knew and didn't—

Dale slammed the glove compartment shut. If he didn't put the keys in the ignition and shift the truck into drive *right now*, he knew he'd do something that Sergeant Simmons would hear about.

Tommy came out of Austin's with his bag. Dale heard himself growl from far away and jerked open the handle of his truck, sliding out onto the ground.

"Hey Tommy?"

Tommy turned around, "What's up?"

Dale closed the distance between them in a few giant strides, closed his fist, and punched him so hard in the jaw that Tommy dropped his food and stumbled backward against the window of the bakery, where the timed lights were just then flickering over the jars of too-early Halloween candy.

Dale's anger dissipated as soon as he blinked to see Tommy righting himself. He covered his own mouth in shock at what he'd done. They stood hunched over, staring, huffing thick steam into the cold morning. Tommy's jaw turned red. He was breathing so hard that his tobacco-black teeth were showing between his lips under an untrimmed mustache.

Dale felt the sickening churn of disbelief in his gut. Instinct made him look around to make sure no one had seen him lose control.

"What the fuck?" Tommy eventually said, sounding more confused than upset. He was the type to get away with most things unscathed, so this was new for him. "I thought you were going to be a cop or some shit?"

"I'm not yet," Dale said, quietly.

Tommy grunted, annoyed, and tested the mobility of his jaw by opening and closing his stained mouth a few times. They watched each other for a little longer to make sure there wasn't going to be a scuffle. A Case harvester puttered over the railroad tracks and onward before Tommy sighed angrily and spoke again.

"Look, okay. Sorry if I was out of line, man, but Gentry was messed up. Wasn't exactly a secret."

Dale exhaled, puffing out his cheeks. He could finally feel his body beginning to return to normal. "Well . . . I'm not going to argue with that." He knelt down and picked up the bag of food with a still-shaking hand. "Here man, let me buy you some more."

"It's all right."

"I'm sorry."

"You're fine. I don't blame you for being raw about it."

"You coming to the funeral?" Dale asked.

"I don't think it would be right. Honestly, I used to do that shit with him back in the day, before he even got hooked."

Dale threw his head back in exasperation, his anger sparking back to life again. "Christ, Tommy. Don't tell me that."

"Gotta think, it probably had Fentanyl, or something, laced or something, I don't know. I get mine from a guy in Fayetteville, and God only knows where he was getting his."

"I'd leave right about now if I were you," Dale said coolly. Tommy scurried toward his truck. "And you either need to get some goddamn sense or move once I get on the force, because that shit isn't going to fly with me, hear?"

"You're the boss, Wyatt Earp," Tommy said bitterly, slamming his truck door.

Dale stood on the sidewalk for several minutes, trembling, eyes burning, face red, muscles still sore from yesterday's shock.

The Mount Zion United Methodist Church didn't even have locks on the doors before Dale was born. Anyone could just walk in, anytime. When they started having to replace the candles and offering plates every six weeks, they decided that keeping the church from going bankrupt should be higher on their list of priorities than "open minds, open hearts, open doors," or at least the last part.

That used to be about as serious as crime got in Bethany. The people were friendly enough, and there didn't seem to be an "illegal substances" problem past the occasional roach in the high-school parking lot and dusty mason jars under sinks for when the beer stopped tasting like anything. Obviously they were wrong.

Dale arrived several hours before the funeral, but didn't plan on staying. He needed to go home and change anyway. The spare key to the little white church was in a magnet hide-a-key against the backside of the air-conditioning unit. He knew this because his mother had been the organist for nearly thirty years, and he knew the little church inside and out. She'd be there any minute to set up for the funeral. The building had comforted him throughout every crisis of his life, but he suddenly found himself wishing he were standing by the dumpsters at the community college, staring down the barrel of a can of mace.

He dropped himself into the back pew and rooted through his Austin's bag, reaching past the fries for his grilled cheese. Yes. Okay. He knew Gentry was getting bad. He'd call Dale and say, "Yeah man. I'm doing good. I've got a job interview lined up . . . it's gonna be good. They're looking for management, lots of positions. It's good. It's gonna be good. I'm getting things straight. Life's too short to fuck around. I just don't want to live the way I been living, know what I mean?" And Dale would say he did know. But what he really knew was what was coming, inevitably, a few weeks later: "Dude, I'm bad, like, I can't get my shit together, you know? I'm about to catch charges from some shit that wasn't even my fault, you know. Is there anything you can, like, I know you're friends with people, is there anything? Man, I stopped going to that shit. The meetings were only making me crazier, you know? They want you to be crazy so you'll keep coming back, that's a fact, so I don't go. Man, if you know anyone who can help me, you let me know, okay?"

Gentry was like a train barreling toward the weak spot in

the tracks, but Dale decided to do the paternal thing and let him learn the hard lessons on his own, and eventually he'd wise up and level out, in good time. But before that, he'd have to hit rock bottom.

Well here we are, man, the voice in his head said. *Rock fucking bottom. Good job.*

After two bites of his grilled cheese, Dale's fingers started to shine with butter. He wiped them on the pew cushion and heard the creaking sound of the front door opening behind him.

"Hello, Mr. Badass."

"Hey, Mama."

Mary Overton sat down beside her son and reached into the bag, pulling out two greasy fries and taking a bite of both. She'd been to the salon and gotten her short hair done in one of those messy things that probably cost forty dollars and two hours of enduring the gossip about Nettie's poor parenting. She was wearing a black dress with tiny white polka dots.

"You look pretty," he said, honestly.

"Wish I had something that was all black."

"I'm sure it'll be fine. Are you playing?"

"Who else are they gonna ask?" she said. Dale liked the relationship he had with his mother. Since his father died of some kind of mental disorder when he was a kid, it had been just the two of them.

She sighed, like you do at the beginning of a big conversation. "I got to Austin's about thirty minutes after you left and talked to Mitchell Canter, up by the window. What'd Tommy say to get under your skin?"

"What if I told you I just felt like hitting him?"

"You know better."

Dale leaned into the back of the pew, sinking a bit deeper

into it with an exaggerated sigh. "Tommy said he wasn't coming to the funeral."

"Ah, I see." Her gray eyes turned devotedly to the cross at the front of the sanctuary. The bag crinkled as she absently reached in for a pinch of his sandwich.

"He just said what everyone's thinking. Have you been to see Nettie?"

"I went last night to clean out her fridge, all the casseroles such, and to talk about the hymns. She's not doing so hot."

"I didn't think so."

She chewed on her cheek for a minute, her eyes watering up. He'd seen women upset before, even Charlie, but nothing was worse to him than his mother losing that tight composure of hers. "You boys . . . same town, same classes, practically under the same roof, practically brothers. Nettie doesn't understand how . . . why you grew up to be who you are and Gentry grew up the way he did."

"I know."

"She came at me while I was cleaning and lost it, hollering, wanting to know what I done right and what she done so wrong. I didn't know what to tell her, because I don't know either. It could have just as easily been you."

He draped his arm around her shoulders. She reached into his bag and blew her nose into a salty napkin, and only then did she seem to snap out of her own head and realize what it was she'd been eating the whole time. "Dale Overton, I know you didn't bring diner food into this church. Get out of here with that."

"Body of Christ broken for you, Mama."

She shook her head, smirking. "I swear to God, son."

He and Charlie arrived back at the church right as the service was starting, moving down the center aisle toward the front of the room, and slipping into the pew behind the Coats' family right as Pastor Ryan started saying the first few words. Nettie turned around to smile halfheartedly at Charlie.

From here, the sharp line of Gentry's nose and the white flat of his forehead peaked over the side of the pearly black casket at the front of the room. Poor Ethan was stuffed into a lumpy suit like clothes in a hefty bag. His odd, wet eyes were wide and confused. There was a faded green stain on the thigh of Charlie's gray dress from a Jell-O shot she'd done at one of Gentry's parties several years ago. His mother was leaned to one side of the organ bench, waiting for the cue from the preacher to start playing. Her hair was already starting to fall flat.

Pastor Ryan said "Amen" and his mother started "the Old Rugged Cross." The pews creaked in agony as everyone stood.

Charlie slid a hymnal from the rack of the pew in front of them, then handed it to him. It was heavier in his hands than he remembered. She leaned over, fumbling with her program during the first few chords. "I didn't hear the number," she hissed.

"504."

She looked at him, shocked. He chuckled. "What? I'm an organist's son." Charlie stared at the hymnal, but he knew the words by heart. "*And I love that old cross, where the dearest and best, for a world of lost sinners was slain.*"

He was thinking about what trophies Gentry had to his name to lay down and how many trophies a person needed to get into Heaven. Several strong, male voices harmonized in the back during the chorus, and he looked around to see the police officers and firefighters of the town in their navy dress uniforms, standing with their backs erect and their heads up, a small militia against grief, a show of order and control guarding Bethany against chaos. Dale wanted to be back there. He wanted to be that.

Instead, he was up front where he didn't belong making an angry wad of the funeral program in his hand. The photo of Gentry on the back, positioned over Psalms 23, was a low-quality image taken from his Facebook page. Earl Coats was falling apart in front of him, and Dale wanted to stand on his own pew and point to Gentry's father and yell something about responsibility and who it belonged to.

He only softened when he felt Charlie shaking with silent sobs beside him. Dale wrapped his arm around her, closing the hymnal that neither of them needed, and pulled her close.

"I will cling to the old rugged cross and exchange it someday for a crown."

"Let us pray."

Dale glanced over his shoulder at the familiar faces behind him: Simmons, the principal of the high school, the gas-station attendant. Even Jackson Hatcher and his weird, secluded family were there. Sarah Hatcher was a nurse at the hospital and their two daughters were odd, to say the least. The youngest had her eyes lifted during the prayer, looking confused, like she'd wandered into the wrong building, like she had never heard of prayer in her life. She met Dale's eyes and gave him an odd, flirtatious look with a wink before the older sister, a beanpole who never spoke, grabbed the top of her head and forced it down. He recalled that both of them knew their way around a Beretta 92 and committed it to memory.

Dale wondered how many of the people behind him had talked mess about Nettie and Gentry on their way to the church.

He wondered if any of them thought about not coming at all, like Tommy Hawthorne, but decided they didn't want to miss the spectacle. He felt them watching the front two rows in fascination, waiting for one or all of them to burst into wild, frenzied hysterics, for Nettie to throw herself into the satin-lined box where Gentry laid with paint on his sunken cheeks, stiff fingers laid over each other, fingers that once reached for her from a crib, fingers that wrapped around his father's thumb when he was learning to walk, fingers that taught Ethan how to play Mario on the basement television when they were all kids, fingers that got burned the day he and Dale started their first bonfire in the backyard. Oh, God.

Pastor Ryan wrapped up the prayer and then entered into a painfully generic speech about the family's love for Gentry, and how Gentry filled everyone around him with joy and love, and how he was brave in his struggle against pain and the world, and now they'd all need to be brave to face a world without his compassion and tenderness.

Dude, don't let them talk about me like I was a fucking pussy.

Charlie and his mother were crying, not for Gentry, as he should've been, but for Nettie. They were crying from a deep, primal place, because a fellow woman was in pain. They were crying because they couldn't imagine losing the thing they loved most in the world, which, he realized now, was *him*.

Dale had once he'd been hit in the eye socket with a baseball at a party, and while he tried to be as much of a man as an eight-year-old could be with a doctor poking at a fractured skull beneath his eyebrow, his mother had stood weeping in the corner of the hospital room, sucking on the knuckles of her right fist. Because that is what mothers do, and wives, and girlfriends, and women. Dale believed it was their gift and their curse to feel the pain of everyone around them.

They would never hesitate to reach out to someone who needed them.

And then, as though confirming the sentiment, Nettie turned around and, unbelievably, reached out and put her hand on Charlie's shoulder, giving her a soft jostle and a pat, comforting her. Comforting *her*.

Dale's suit was strangling him. The temperature had risen at least ten degrees since they'd arrived from all the breathing bodies.

They put makeup on me, man. I have lipstick on. I'm going into the hole like a fucking drag queen. That's what they ought to be crying about. You believe this shit?

Dale leapt to his feet in the middle of the Lord's Prayer, angry as he'd been when he punched Tommy on the sidewalk. His father had been prone to episodes of agitation like this, and now he finally understood what it felt like, like being the only person standing in the middle of a crowded church during your best friend's funeral with the entire town watching to see what you'll do next.

He whipped himself around and marched down the center aisle, out the back doors of the church just as everyone said "Amen." Dale kicked up dust as he marched to Charlie's truck and kicked the tire, causing a funny ricochet of his dress shoe against the black rubber. He opened the driver's door and slammed it shut. He opened the door again, climbed inside, and knocked his hands on the steering wheel once, twice, three times. He couldn't stop and he didn't care. It was a proper temper tantrum.

He spent the next fifteen minutes concentrating in the driver's seat, trying to recall a dream, trying to see a shape in one of those scattered 3D pictures. He waited for the voice in his head to say anything: "I forgive you. I hate you. I needed you. How could you. Fuck you. I love you." Anything at all.

Finally, Charlie snuck out of the side door of the church as the two front doors opened, pallbearers struggling under Gentry's heavy weight. She click-clacked down the sidewalk and then crunched over the gravel to get to him. He climbed out of the truck and went to the opposite side, so the truck bed stretched between them. There were a few cups from Austin's and some black bungee cords that clattered around whenever they took a turn too hard.

Her head dropped about three inches. She must have taken her heels off, because he could hear her toes shifting a little on the hard gravel as she lowered her head to the metal on the side of the truck bed. The woman could dance on coals if she had to. He hoped she never would. Dale stared at the top of her head and sighed, feeling incredibly enamored and desperately affectionate toward her.

"I love you," he said.

Charlie lifted her head. The warm metal left a faint red mark on her face that would linger for a while. "I love you," she said, with her calm, earnest, tear-stained gaze.

Dale felt the burn on his scalp from the pepper spray, exaggerated by the sun overhead, and the burn in his eyes *not* from the tear gas, and the bruised snakebite on his arm from the Taser, which is better than pepper spray because when it's over, it's over.

They climbed into the truck, and he accidentally mashed the gas pedal too hard, kicking rocks up as he left the Mount Zion United Methodist Church parking lot heading toward the cemetery of their God-forsaken town. This God-forsaken community that he was about to dedicate his life to protect. This God-forsaken place and these God-forsaken people that he needed to learn how to love.

Be good, man.

VALLEY OF THE SHADOW

IT WAS THREE YEARS LATER WHEN Nettie Coats woke up after her eldest son's funeral to find herself sitting on the porch with a man she met on the internet. She was staring absently at a guinea hen in the yard when she looked over and saw him—Richard, maybe?—in the rocking chair next to her, one of a pair that her long-gone husband had made for their twentieth anniversary. The man was not what she would call handsome. He was in his mid-fifties like her, but rocking back and forth like a child, grinning stupidly at the yard in front of them.

"This is just charming," he said. "What an absolutely charming homestead. I'm so glad we decided to do this."

No one had ever referred to her ten acres as a "homestead" before. Nettie looked around, a little bit dazed. Empty dirt dauber nests stuck to the upper framework of the porch like pan-pipes. The white paint was peeling from the rails. Weeds had overtaken the front walk, swallowing the burgundy irises her late grandmother had transplanted from the family's old farm in the mountains before it was sold. Everything around her seemed thirsty. Even the skin of her palms and fingers was scaly and split from working the farm by herself, often causing her sudden pain.

"This is so wonderful," Richard said, gleefully. "And everyone here is so polite. I noticed that at my hotel. You don't get that where I'm from."

"Can I get you something to drink?" she asked, wearily.

"How about a refreshing mint julep?" he said, dead serious.

"Does this look like Twelve Oaks to you?"

The stupid grin never left his face. "Never heard of it."

She leaned her head back against the old wood of the rocking chair. "I think I have green Evan and Coors Light in the fridge."

"Please, madam. Whatever you recommend."

She prayed he was making fun of her.

Nettie stood up and walked across the dry-rotted boards into the house, resisting the urge to slam the door. She could blame all of this on her twenty-four-year-old son. About a year ago, Ethan told her he'd found a forum on the internet for divorced parents who had lost a child. She was in her armchair in the living room, toying with a magazine that she wasn't reading. Nettie could tell it took a great deal of courage for Ethan to climb the stairs from his sanctuary in the basement and speak to her directly. "If you're ready, when you're ready, or whenever . . . I emailed you the link. You can get to it on your laptop. You could give it a try." She was silent. He said, "At some point," and retreated back to the world he'd created for himself downstairs. They said that he was perfectly healthy—just a perfectly healthy man who had not stepped foot out of the basement in two years, who required his dinner to be delivered, who bought a minifridge and microwave last year. He'd created an entire life in a hole, but the good news, the doctor said, was that he just needed to go see someone. That was the issue. He needed to go to a psychiatrist. He needed to go.

But if Ethan wanted her to try, she would try. Not much good it did her. Now there was an awkward man with a stutter on her front porch.

She popped a Coors for herself and dropped two ice cubes into a blue plastic cup with "Earl's Auto Services & Supply: If We Can't Fix It, You Shouldn't Drive It" stamped on the side. It was some cheap promotional stunt that Earl's right-hand man, Jackson Hatcher, had come up with. They tried handing them out at the town's tobacco festival last year, but most of them had ended up in her cabinet, occasionally spilling out onto the floor no matter how many times she tried to stack them behind the glasses and mugs.

She gave Richard the rest of the bottle of Evans, about three shot's worth, and she *did* slam the door on her way out.

He smiled. "Drafty, huh?"

There was something wrong with him. She had not been aware enough to notice it when he drove from the university town on the other side of the state last month to have coffee with her, but it was painfully obvious now. Nettie gave him Earl's plastic cup.

"I'm not promising it'll taste like it does wherever you come from," she said.

He looked worried. "I'm from Providence, remember?"

"Well, wherever. Shit." Things were starting to come back to her, slowly.

"Have you ever seen Providence?" he asked.

"Not lately," she said, slurping foam. Nettie had the sudden horrifying thought that the divorce papers were still on the kitchen table, under stacks of Ethan's video game magazines and unopened bills and slips of paper with Bible verses on them that arrived every month inside of the care packages from the Mount Zion United Methodist Church down the road. She had not been to church since before Gentry died, and didn't know why they kept pestering her.

If the divorce papers were still on the table, it meant that Richard might see them. She wondered if she cared and decided she didn't. He'd gotten divorced shortly after his daughter died—an innocent girl caught in the crossfire of a drug dispute over heroin in front of a grocery store while she was putting produce in the back of her car. Gentry had died from heroin, too.

"So, have you ever been on a farm?" she asked, trying to sound curious.

"Yes, of course," he nodded. "When I traveled abroad each year, I stayed at an inn in Switzerland that was near a dairy farm. They did tours every day for visitors."

"No real farm has tours," she said under her breath.

"So, how many animals do you have?" Richard asked.

"Twenty-one goats, three horses, six guineas, two dogs, and a cat."

He sipped the whiskey. "Hmm . . . that's good."

"Glad you think so," she laughed.

"You know, you don't sound at all like I imagined you might."

"I don't talk like the Queen of England." She sat up straight and held her beer like it was a wine glass, obnoxiously imitating his speech patterns: "Oh, please, madam, get me whatever champagne you have just lying around. Charming, charming. Mint juleps. I'm from Providence, and I travel to the low countries every Christmas to study old buildings."

"It was January," he said, completely unfazed. "And the Low Countries are the Netherlands and Belgium, mostly—"

"Fine," she said.

"Some parts of Germany, depending on who you're talking to."

"Good for you."

All of the things that had not seemed worth doing around the farm over the last three years seemed worth doing now, if it would make him leave. She wanted to wash the dishes. She wanted to wipe down the windows. Quit smoking. Have Ethan teach her how to play the game he and Gentry liked to play together, when Gentry was alive, the one with the taxi cabs and the drug smuggling and the hookers you could stab.

He laughed. "I saw a sign the other day for a restaurant off the highway, with chicken livers as the special. Can you believe that?"

"I can," she said. "Chicken livers are good, if you do them right."

For the first time, he looked shocked. "Oh. I hadn't given it much thought. Southerners have a strange preoccupation with food, don't they?"

"If you'd lay off of your crumpets and try some—"

"You *do* know that New England isn't actually England, right?"

"Try our food then tell me it's not better than food anywhere else."

"I've had a fair sampling of it."

"Have you ever had Hopping John?"

"No."

"Chow-Chow?"

"No."

"Brunswick stew?"

"I have heard of Brunswick stew."

"Ever had it?"

"Well actually," he said, thoughtfully. "No."

"All right then."

"I'm learning so much," he said, delighted. He liked to learn, she could tell. Richard was a professor of architecture at the university. He traveled all over creation with students to point at piles of bricks and arches and churches as big as castles. As it stood, she was too attached to her house, empty and broken down as it was. Just like Ethan with his basement, she could never leave this town, especially not now, when it cradled the bones of her boy deep in its red clay.

"You like to learn?" she said, suddenly depressed. "Here's something. Do you know why we paint the porch ceilings blue in the South?"

He looked up. "I do not."

"It confuses the birds and bugs. They don't build nests in the sky."

He went back to his hotel at dusk, but not before insisting on tagging along with her for church the next day. She tried telling him that she didn't go to church, but it didn't seem to occur to him to let her have a choice, just like she didn't have a choice before he called her with news that he was staying at the Holiday Inn by the highway for the weekend.

"Surprise!" he had said.

If her husband were there, she knew exactly what he'd say about the situation: "fucked up beyond all recognition." FUBAR.

There was no Catholic presence in the small town of Bethany, so they had to settle for Mount Zion. She pulled on her black blouse, the one with the silver sequins on the collar.

She'd considered sending Richard to fend for himself, but the Congregational Care Committee had a habit of harassing newcomers, and she didn't want him blabbing to the who town about her business. Nettie had gone through a lot of trouble to maintain her anonymity over the last three years. It was better if *she* could say what needed saying if they got asked, instead of trusting him to not say the wrong thing. Hopefully they'd leave them both alone.

He pulled up in her driveway at ten-thirty so they could make the eleven o'clock service. The sun was suspended over the frost like a white bulb on a cord, and the animals were out in what little warmth it was providing. Earl's two beagles, Roscoe and Pooter, were sprawled on a flat rock sticking out of the ground.

"We can take my car," he said, excitedly.

"No."

"Why?"

Nettie was already getting into her truck. "If you drive a black ass Mustang through *this* town—"

"People might stare?" he said, smiling, giving her a nudge as he walked by. "That's the point."

"You're too damn old to be acting like a teenager. Get in the truck or walk," she said. He visibly deflated. His excitement was grating to her, his voice even more so. It was different from the northerners she'd met coming in and out of town. Richard's voice was wooden, too formal, his intonation unbearably repetitive. And where he should have been offended, he smiled. Where sentences were simple, he stuttered.

Awkward. That was the only word for him. Awkward.

Almost on cue, he said, "I *do* wish you'd let me take you for a little spin at some point."

"Why do you talk like that?" she asked, unable to hold it in any longer. She started up the truck and backed it out of the driveway.

"Like what?"

"Like a robot with a stick up its ass."

"Oh, yes," he laughed. "I supposed I should've led with this. I was diagnosed with autism when I was in my forties." She'd only heard the term a few times in her life, but she figured it must have something to do with over-sharing. "My forties!" he laughed. "Imagine that! A grown man! My mother thought it was obvious, but my wife, especially after our daughter died—"

"I get the picture," Nettie said, not in the mood.

"—after our daughter died, my wife found it hard to accommodate both her grief and my condition. Things changed in our marriage drastically after we lost Emily." He'd obviously given this speech to a few therapists before her. It sounded rehearsed. "She said it was easy when she had a child to distract her, but once she didn't, it got unbearable for her. She was an easygoing type and I'm . . . well, you see how I am. But I'm trying to get better . . . to loosen my tie, if you will."

"I will," she said.

"And actually, the peculiar part is that, if I think about it, and according to my therapist, Emily likely had some form of autism as well."

Nettie rumpled her forehead, squinting into the sun. "Autism."

"Yes."

She took the curves in the road smoothly, thinking of Ethan in the basement of her house, glued to a screen, making his money doing God-only-knows-what, going weeks only speaking to virtual people. Autism was one of the things his doctors had "ruled out." It wasn't something that got talked about when she was growing up, but she figured it was just another word for people who "weren't quite right," as her father used to say. That seemed more likely than there being a sudden epidemic.

When they arrived at church, Richard practically skipped down the aisle into the front row, closest to the pulpit. Nettie considered sitting in the back where she was less conspicuous, but she sat next to the poor guy anyway.

"What a charming little place," he said of the one-room chapel with splintering wooden pews. "Charming. So charming."

People filed in—people she hadn't seen since Gentry's funeral three years ago—wearing giant work coats over their dresses and suits.

"Just adorable," he said, still grinning.

"Don't you study cathedrals in Europe and shit?" she whispered.

"I study sacred spaces. This is a *sacred* space."

She sighed. "Not for me."

The pews were full of people now, and she could feel them staring at the back of her head wondering about "Nettie's new man." The joys and concerns and announcements were of births, deaths, cancer screenings, rehearsal for the Christmas cantata, and one little kid who raised his hand and asked for prayers for his indoor hockey game. That was new. If there'd been indoor hockey league when Gentry was a boy, he would've been all over it.

Richard stumbled through the Apostles' Creed and in a few places of the Lord's Prayer, but he kept up pretty well with the Protestant service otherwise. She nearly fell over with embarrassment when he crossed himself, and again when he dropped a check for a hundred dollars into the collection plate. He smiled at her proudly like he'd just tipped a waiter two-hundred percent.

Other than that, Nettie did not openly acknowledge the man in the gray Italian suit at all during the service. The organist, Mary, a long-time friend of Nettie's, kept eying her with mischievous suspicion between hymns, making faces and wagging her eyebrows. Mary's son was sitting near the front with his spunky wife, Charlotte—a girl that Nettie adored in spite of her husband.

Dale Overton met her gaze and gave her a small, sheepish smile that she did not return. He'd lost a lot of weight. His face was gaunt and pale and his eyes had a strange, crazed look in them. Maybe he was just anxious to see her for the first time in a while.

She suddenly recognized that *he* was the biggest reason she rarely went into town—not because she was afraid of him, but because she was afraid of what she'd do *to* him if given the opportunity.

Dale had been Gentry's best friend from the time they could speak right up until Dale got it in his bloated head that he wanted to be a police officer. Then he was suddenly too good to be seen around her heroin-addicted son. Dale married Charlie and distanced himself from Gentry when he needed support the most. Pastor Ryan's generic, between-liturgical-seasons sermon about forgiveness made Nettie feel attacked, or at the very least, a very poor candidate for whatever providence the building had to offer.

On the way home, Richard said, "The child that sang the solo in the choir could very well become a stage singer, one day. She was phenomenal." Nettie didn't answer, so he commenced to talking about opera—this one in Vienna and that one in Paris. He used back-of-the-DVD words like "phenomenal" and "sensational" and "ravishing" and "captivating."

"My wife was Baptist," he said when it was clear she was not musically inclined enough to comment on Andrew Lloyd Webber. "Are Baptists quite different from Methodists?"

"I don't know. Earl—my . . . ex-husband" it was the first time she'd said it out loud, "He grew up Baptist."

"Was Earl a lot like you?"

"If he were my father he'd have spit me out of his mouth," she said.

He hooted and slapped his leg with laughter.

"Gentry was just like me, though," she said suddenly. Richard fell quiet. "Hard-headed and soft-hearted."

"I wouldn't say you have a soft heart."

Nettie was surprised to hear it, especially from him. Of course she had a soft heart. Instantly indignant, she began thinking about all the nice things she'd done for people recently. She didn't come up with much.

She barely tapped the brakes at the stop sign in front of Earl's Auto Services & Supply and kept going through the empty intersection. It'd been closed for almost three years since Earl left; she had made no effort to keep his business going, and no one had set a foot in it since. It was starting to show its disuse. Maybe the nicest thing her family had done for the people of Bethany was remove themselves from their gazes entirely, each in their own way.

"Things used to hurt Gentry," she said, quieter. "He didn't like watching the news or reading too many books. He had an empathy problem."

"Sympathy."

"What's the difference?"

"Sympathy means you understand what people go through and you feel bad for their misery," he said like he was reading from a dictionary. "Empathy means you put yourself in the shoes of another person."

"Well hell, he had both," she said.

The hens were strutting around in front of the house when they got home. Richard watched them with some anxiety. "Are those turkeys?"

"Guinea hens," she said, turning off the truck. "Just kick them if they get too close."

"Didn't you say you had a cat? Does it not attack the hens?" He didn't seem to understand that he was asking too many damn questions and she was getting tired of answering them.

"Not usually. He stays in the barn and eats enough rats to stay full."

"Do the hens lay eggs?"

"No. They eat the ticks."

"That's all they do?"

"Guineas eat the ticks so the ticks don't eat me," she said, climbing the stairs.

"Out of curiosity, then . . . where do you get eggs?"

"The grocery store," she answered. "Lord, boy."

After eating the McDonald's they'd picked up on the way home, she gave him a short tour of her home, as opposed to keeping him sequestered in the same three rooms she used. He discovered her mother's old Lester upright in the dining room and began picking out various hymns and pieces he'd learned as a child, songs that made her feel cold and nostalgic and lonely. She started out leaned against a doorframe, listening, then started wandering the rooms in her house, rooms that had become strange to her, pushing years of papers and mess back and forth with her fingers as though discovering it all for the first time.

He asked for a beer as the sun started going down, probably hoping she wouldn't send him back to the hotel again when he was leaving the next day.

"That's all I have left since you polished off my Evans," she said. She brought the entire case of Coors into the living room. There were only a handful left. She pounded two quickly, in the hopes that it might help her relax and enjoy his company in her sanctuary, her space. The living room of the old farmhouse was full of junk; that was the only word she could think of to describe it, now that she was seeing it all through a stranger's eyes—junk piled into corners, stacked on top of the television, stuffed into the magazine rack beside the couch, all over the walls. There were dreamcatchers, glued Thomas Kincaid puzzles on cardboard in and out of frames, ribbons from various county fairs, three separate clocks above her fireplace—two grandmothers and a Regulator each stopped dead on a different time. She must've looked like a hoarder to him. Maybe she was.

There were five photos on her mantel: a broad-shouldered Appaloosa, a red goat with a dusty white face, the two beagles sitting on the outside porch, a young boy with acne, and a teenage boy with glasses giving what she had always hoped was just a sideways peace sign. All of the photos, except for one, were printed from her computer on plain letter paper with a knick-knack of some sort holding it in place; the goat's was high quality and shining, framed, with a second-place ribbon attached to the top right-hand corner. There was a stereo in the corner constantly rotating six different Dolly Parton CDs, even throughout the night.

With every swallow, Nettie sank deeper into her green arm-chair. She watched Richard wandering around, poking at things in amazement. He walked to the shelf above the stereo system, and picked up the box set that was laying open.

"Do you like Dolly Parton?" he asked.

"Damn. I was hoping I could keep it a secret."

He didn't catch the sarcasm and slurped his beer. "She has big boobs," he said.

"Is that all you know about her?" she asked, turning on an old lamp by the chair and leaning back. It cast a sad, dim yellow light. She tucked her legs beneath her to keep her feet warm.

"I know she wrote that one song."

"She's written literally about three thousand. One of them is the saddest song on earth."

"Which is . . . ?"

"It's called 'Daddy Come and Get Me'."

"May I hear it?" Richard asked.

"It'll make me cry."

He put the discs down where he found them and sat down on the couch. "Emily liked country music . . . or western music, if there's a difference."

"There is," Nettie said.

"When I used to take my students abroad every winter, Emily would always travel with me. Not on the school's dime, but alongside me and my students, you see."

"How sweet."

"Every year for fifteen years . . . and Emily was quite a sight, let me tell you, bee-bopping through metro stations in France and Germany and cathedrals listening to her headphones with Reba McEntire and George Strait and Johnny Cash. Maybe some Dolly Parton, too," he laughed. "But I think she got bored.

She'd seen all the cathedrals before."

"Every year for fifteen years," Nettie echoed, to prove she was listening.

"Emily loved the churches in Paris. French Gothic was her thing." The beer was causing him to lose control of his stutter, which gave his voice a jerking tremble every few syllables that he punctuated with a compulsive cough. "I couldn't even get her to enjoy German Gothic, no matter how hard I tried. I don't understand how anyone could like St. Denis but not Cologne. I'm not sure where I went wrong with her."

"Kids are the darnedest things." It was starting to feel pointless even trying to mock him.

Richard looked at her, happy for the validation. "Aren't they?" He polished his beer and pointed at her with it, narrowing his eyes. "I got her good, though, Nettie. I got her good."

"Yeah?" Now she was actually curious.

"The last trip we did together, before the, you know, I took the students to Spain. But we didn't usually go to Spain. Usually it was Italy, Germany, and France. But I dragged them to Spain, to Barcelona, and showed them the Sagrada Familia."

"Wow," she said.

"It's a Roman Catholic minor basilica in Barcelona," he said.

"What's a minor basilica?"

"A church that's usually under some kind of extra protection from the Vatican, the Pope."

"Is that a cathedral, too?"

"No. Cathedrals are a bigger deal. That's where the bishops sit over their dioceses."

"Sit," she said.

"Yeah. Cathedral literally means 'sit down' in Greek," he said, laughing a little bit. She imagined an old man in a colorful hat with a beard sitting on a throne. It was what God looked like to her.

"Churchs, basilicas, cathedrals," she said. He was like a walking documentary.

Richard said, "And the funny thing is that the Sagrada Familia isn't even finished."

"How long do these things take to build?" she asked.

"Oh, it won't be done until about 2030."

"Well shit, how long have they been working on it?" She leaned forward.

"Since about 1880."

"Damn."

"So yeah. I took Emily and my students in there, on a sunny day, and as soon as she saw those stained glass windows . . . man, she was done for. The headphones fell off of her head and hit the floor behind her and she instantly started crying." His hands were beginning to shake, so he shoved them between his knees like a child.

"Do you want another beer?" she asked, concerned.

"No, I think I'm fine. Anyway, Emily told me later that it was like being inside a kaleidoscope. And that's a good way to put it. She always did have a thing for words like that."

"So she saw the colors and cried?" Nettie asked.

Richard was staring off, his excitement drained. "Yeah. She saw the colors and cried."

Nettie would have liked to see colors that powerful. She wanted to be inside a kaleidoscope. She'd like to cry. It was the right time for it. A man in her living room, by the fire, him talking about his dead daughter and the things she loved about the world, forcing her to remember her dead son and all the things he hated about it. Her heart was opening, wasn't it? Is this what it felt like?

She pulled down an old shawl from the back of the chair and wrapped it around her shoulders, feeling very elderly, curled in her chair, staring at the fire while he snapped out of his reverie and spoke of transepts and naves and Our Ladies of Mercy and Brunelleschi's dome. There was a cathedral nicknamed "God's Lantern" in a town called Metz in France because it had the largest stained glass collection in the world. There were apparently mosques that used to be churches, which used to be pagan temples—the same ground, recycled over and over, never demolished but simply covered with something else, another monument to another thing, something else to worship. He explained that sometimes cathedral workers had to spend more time cleaning up the wreckage from fallen attempts at cathedrals than they did actually building one, until they discovered the idea of buttresses. Then the French took up the idea of *flying* buttresses, which served the same purpose but looked better doing it. "I got into more arguments with my daughter about this than I care to admit. I appreciate their function academically, but they look so tacky to me. But her being so damn defensive of her French architecture—" He hung his head.

There it is, Nettie thought. The moment they'd been waiting for.

Richard inhaled. "Can I tell you something?" he asked.

"Sure," Nettie said, in a voice that she hoped sounded empathetic or sympathetic or both.

"I think I miss my wife more than I miss my child."

Nettie leaned back, chest deflating. She thought about Earl's empty dresser drawers and Gentry's Dodge parked in the barn, and tried to figure out which one hurt worse, but to her dismay, she realized neither of them caused her the same punched-in-the-gut feeling they used to. She could not put her finger on the moment when Gentry's bedroom had become "the guest room," or when she figured out that Earl wasn't coming back and she might as well use the old flannel shirts he left behind for working in the barn. She couldn't remember the moments the people on the online forums called *pivotal*. Maybe she had never pivoted at all. Maybe she'd been moving in a straight line this whole time, and the world had pivoted around her.

"I don't know who I miss more—my husband or my boy," she said. "And I think that's fine. I mean, I don't think anyone's got any right to tell you it's *not* fine. I think you and I have gone into some place where the world's logic and shit can't go, a dark place under everything else, like Hell."

"Or a basement," he said, looking at her.

She felt angry for a split second, thinking it was a jab at the only child she had left, but Richard was not the type for low blows. He was kinder than her by far. She'd give him that.

Her eyes started going wet. "What's wrong with him?" she pleaded.

Richard leaned back against the couch. "It's called agora-phobia," he said.

"Agoraphobia."

"It's a crippling fear of leaving a space that you think is safe."

Fear, she thought. Fear was good. Fears could be overcome. "Is that all? Well if he's anything like me and Earl, he'll power through it."

"I'm afraid phobias don't work that way. They're a little more complicated than just regular fears. He needs help. He needs therapy, maybe anti-anxiety medications. They even have doctors that will come to your house—"

"Not around here," she said, desperate. "I've looked. There's a loony bin at the hospital where Sarah Hatcher works with the crazy people, and I tried to get her to ask someone, but there's some jurisdiction bullshit, and there's not a system in place for it."

"Well," Richard said. "Then you're in a pickle. I'll not deny that. But me . . . I can't be anything other than what I am, Nettie. I can try to manage my mind and fight against it, but this is me. You can't therapy your way out of autism. You can only accept it as part of your identity. But you can therapy your way out of a phobia. It doesn't have to be part of who you are. And it's not a *loony bin*. It's called a *psychiatric inpatient facility.*"

"Psyche ward," she said.

"That's a little better, I guess."

Nettie shivered and considered building a fire in the fireplace that should've been swept of its ashes a long time ago. Ethan had a space-heater downstairs, and she preferred her armchair anyway, so she generally kept the heat off in the autumn for as long as she could stand it.

If Earl had his way, they would've never run it. The man burned 110 degrees by default. Gentry was the same way, inside and out. They went stomping around here and there with their tempers, burning people up. Sometimes they'd explode on one another for lack of anyone else to explode onto. They'd take it out into the yard and yell it out, most of the time about nothing at all. Gentry's dirty room, Earl's then-failing garage, Gentry's ungratefulness, Earl's drinking, Gentry's shady friends—one flung fireball after another while Nettie and Ethan watched from the kitchen, trying not to laugh. It wasn't even a love-hate relationship. Gentry loved Earl and Earl loved that boy. Earl missed his boy more than he wanted her.

Nettie looked up at Richard and realized that he was looking at her. Evaluating her.

"Do you need another beer?" he asked.

"I think we both need to be done."

Richard was drunk on Coors of all things (how was it possible to be drunk off of Coors?), and she didn't want him driving, didn't want his blood on her hands. Nettie offered him the guest room, where her son's deep-blue, tattered bedspread had been folded in the closet and replaced with her mother's yellow quilt. He took her up on it. She gave him one of Earl's shirts—her work shirts—and walked him down the hallway to the room that still haunted her youngest son years after walking up on Gentry's cold body, but did not haunt her anymore.

She turned off all the lights and fell onto her bed like a half-done pancake on a skillet, even spreading a few inches. She felt the presence of a son and the presence of a man in her house, as tangible as heat in the air. It was a peaceful feeling, one she had not realized that she still missed. Nettie closed her eyes and fell into the first real sleep she'd had in years.

The sympathetic "I know there's nothing I can say" phone calls and cards stopped coming about three weeks after Gentry's death. She stopped getting invited to church socials, or coffee, or lunch at Austin's. No more "Do you need any help around the house? I can send my boys over." No more Jell-O molds or casseroles or pasta salads to throw out to the goats. It made her feel as though her allotted period of mourning had run its course. She was in overtime now, and people had already lost interest in her and her grief. She didn't have to sit at Austin's diner and listen to know how this worked.

After a few days, they were saying, "You hear about Gentry Coats? My God. Horrible."

Two weeks later, they were saying, "So sad about that poor boy of Nettie's."

A month, and it was, "Has anyone checked in on her recently? I meant to, but—"

A year, and "What was his name again? Wasn't that Nettie's kid?"

Three years, she didn't know. Didn't want to know.

Since Richard's arrival she had begun to wonder if the help had stopped coming because people had abandoned her, or because she made it abundantly clear that help wasn't wanted. *Was* it? If she reached out right now to Pastor Ryan, or Mary Overton, or her other son equally forgotten by the world in the basement . . . would they come? What would she even ask of them? "Please put my skeleton back together. Please wrap the muscles around the bones. Please stretch my skin over all of it. Please put my boy back into the hips he broke and let me try again."

Never once did Nettie collapse into a dramatic fit of tears at the altar like other people in the town to say, "I am grieving. Bring me potato salad." Her wailing and gnashing of teeth happened in the bread aisle as she thought, isn't it nice only buying groceries for a family of two instead of a family of four? At least now she can have Vitamin-D milk instead of skim, sharp cheddar instead of mild, Wheaties instead of Cheerios.

Pastor Ryan used a particular verse at Floyd Underwood's funeral; she couldn't recall the specifics now, maybe Romans, but it used the words "groans," which wasn't a word she heard from the pulpit very often and always reminded her of something primal.

There was something primal about her grief. She certainly felt like an animal when she dragged herself up the stairs every night, sick from the hiss-crack-pop of beers being opened. Those moments made her think of screaming widows and mothers in ancient worlds, tearing their clothes and ripping their hair. Maybe she would have done that if she thought anyone would hear her, crazy lady in her big house on her *homestead*. Small town. Big grief. Small bottles. One at a time. Put the glass in the recycle. Recycle. Reuse the sacred ground and rebuild the cathedral walls. Give the buttresses wings.

"The Holy Spirit knows what we need, even when we're hurting so much that all we can do is groan. He is enough for you. And you are enough for Him."

Every now and then she remembered that verse and the moment she first heard it. Every now and then, those particular words came to her mind and sat just a little bit higher than the occasional whooshing of precious ghosts in her mind. The verse sat patiently, waiting to be noticed. It sat, and whispered the word *"Enough"* until the soft syllables faded into a dark, sleepy haze.

Nettie rode to Austin's the next morning and bought a few biscuits and coffee. She wanted to do something special for Richard before he left. She asked for a sausage biscuit and orange juice for Ethan, because that was always his favorite. She felt very accomplished and very maternal when she knocked on the basement door and passed the white paper bag from the top of the stairs to where he stood, five steps down. He turned immediately and went back downstairs. "Feels like I'm feeding a troll," she said to his back, a poor attempt at humor. He didn't respond and closed the door, leaving her feeling instantly guilty.

She was eating her biscuit on the porch and slipping ham

to Roscoe—who was suddenly showing signs of aging—when Richard came out quietly and sat down, the rocking chair creaking under his weight. She wondered what she would do if it broke into splinters. Firewood, maybe.

"Good morning," she said, passing him the bag. "Breakfast?"

"Oh, thank you. Yes. This will be good, before I get on the road."

She looked out at the tree-line on the far side of the field and saw where the sun was finally starting to peel through the fog, turning it a strange, dusty yellow. There was a surprising and eerie silence enveloping the land around them.

"You ever thought about how it feels to die?" Nettie asked suddenly.

Richard gave a rare pause. "I think every parent who has lost a child has considered that at one point or another."

"What'd you come to?"

"What I hope or what I think?"

"Hope," she said.

"Have you ever been put under anesthesia for a surgery?" he asked. "Like that."

Nettie thought about heroin laced with Fentanyl and imagined Gentry in his final moments, sprawled onto the floor, drifting to sleep, perhaps wondering which cereal he was going to eat when he woke up—her child, slipping away without even knowing he was leaving, without the opportunity to see the sun again, or pray, or shake his father's hand. She had to physically flinch to get the sight out of her mind.

"I don't think there are any good ways to die," Richard said, not even noticing her discomfort. "I suppose that there are ways I certainly would NOT want to die."

"How's that?"

"Being buried alive."

She let the one bad thought chase away the one that was worse. "How else?"

"Drowning, right?"

"I don't think drowning would be so bad."

"Or being burned alive. At the stake, you know."

"That would suck," she said. "What is it that Queen Elizabeth used to do?"

"Beheading?"

"No. The other thing. Where you cut someone up."

"Drawn and quartered. Now that would suck." The word seemed unfamiliar in his mouth.

"What about something fun?"

"A fun way to die?"

"Taking a cyanide pill and jumping out of an airplane."

He took a second to develop a mental image. "Or smoking too much weed."

"Can that actually kill you?" she asked.

"I don't know," he admitted. "Never smoked."

"Driving a four-wheeler off the Grand Canyon," she suggested, gaining momentum.

"You're all about dying via gravity, aren't you?"

"Pop Rocks and Coke and jumping jacks," she chuckled, her voice hoarse in the cold. "Or snitching on the mob. You'd be everyone's hero for about an hour."

Richard snorted. "Getting drunk and driving as fast as you can into an AA meeting?"

Nettie laughed out loud like a controlled explosion. She kicked her feet up slightly, sending her rocking chair backward before it pitched her forward again, head in her lap. She looked up and saw Richard watching her in joyful disbelief.

"Lord have mercy," she said, still smiling.

"Lord have mercy."

He left late that afternoon with an awkward, back-patting hug and a few lines like: "I'll be talking to you" and a "Travel safe" and a "I could come back for Christmas?" and a "We'll see" and a "Or you could come to me?" and another "We'll see." Richard put his leather duffel and suit bag in the trunk, then climbed down into the car and shut the door. He rolled down the window like folks do when they want to keep talking but it's also time to go.

Nettie gestured to the horizon. "You know, you're kind of like a cowboy. Riding off into the sunset."

He smiled. "Like Dolly would sing about."

Once he was gone, she stood on the cold porch and stared at the place where his car had disappeared.

Then she cleaned the kitchen. She washed the dirty pots with her hands. Three or four of them had to be taken out into the yard and sprayed with the hose. Nettie stripped pages out of magazines and crumbled up old mail and even tore up the Bible verses from the years of monthly care packages and took them into the living room for fire-fodder. She went out and fed her animals and then Nettie Coats used her clean kitchen to make spaghetti. She had no meat and no sauce and no cheese. What she had was a two-year-old can of Ro-tel that she dumped onto the noodles with salt.

She made a plate and leaned against the doorframe at the top of the basement stairs, trying to gather her thoughts.

"Ethan?" she finally said. A sudden shuffle, some clacking of plastic, the sound of office-chair wheels on the concrete floor downstairs.

"Mama?" he said. "You call me?"

"Can I come down?" she asked.

"Uhh, yeah. That's fine."

She went down the stairs for the first time in months. It was his basement now. He had been receiving mysterious shipments to the back door for a while, and now she could see why.

The concrete floor was painted with a shiny garage coat of gray, and there was an old coffee table by the tiny bathroom with a microwave, a hot plate, and a mini-fridge on it. The bed in the corner was neatly made with green sheets, and there was an exercise machine of some kind with bells and whistles that she couldn't have figured out if she tried. But the most incredible thing was Ethan himself. He was leaned back in his office chair, two screens in front of him, talking into an orange microphone on the desk.

"AFK," he said, and then pulled his ear-buds out.

He turned to her, raising an eyebrow. The last time she had seen him—*really* seen him, in the light of the world—he had been a doughy, nerdy kid with acne and a bowl cut. Now her son's chin was angled out, God, like Earl's, and his shoulders were bulkier. He wore a plain white shirt that exposed his muscular arms. She couldn't believe how much healthier he looked with his entire world contained in a space half the size of a volleyball court. Hair trimmed, smooth skin, and peaceful eyes. "Well, hey," Ethan said, a tilted little smile on his face.

"Hey, you."

He leaned back in his chair and took the plate of spaghetti she offered him. "So," he drew the syllable out with his mouth full, acknowledging the eighteen elephants in the room. He went with the most obvious first, as she would have. "So, I heard a visitor up there. You finally gettin' some after all these years?" His eyes were mischievous.

"Oh, you shut your mouth," she said. She sank down on the

couch. "It was your idea anyway."

"Hey, don't put it off on me."

They laughed, and she prepared herself while his fork clanked against the plate. But instead of the speech she'd decided upon, she couldn't stop herself from blurting out, "How'd you do all this, anyway? All by yourself?"

"Youtube and WikiHow, mostly. Trial and error and time. I've got lots of time."

"And money?"

"I play video games for a living."

"Come again?"

"I play, and people watch because I'm good at it." He pointed to the screen where a game was paused. "And I teach people how to be good at playing theirs. They donate."

"So it's like a performance."

He shrugged. "I was playing the games anyway."

"Can I ask you something else?"

He nodded.

"Why don't you leave the basement, son?"

He sighed, like he'd been waiting for this and dreading it for a while. "I like it down here," he said. She fought her urge to say something smarmy and waited for him to answer her—really answer her. "I think . . . I think it's some kind of, like, anxiety, or something."

"It's arachnophobia," she said gravely.

He pushed his lips together like he was trying not to laugh. "I don't think it's arachnophobia, Mama. That's spiders."

"You know what I mean."

"I know what you mean." His smile faded and he wiped the corner of his mouth with his thumb. "It's just that, up there is kind of a different place now. To me. In my head. It's not really my house. It's not really our house. I mean, maybe it was. But it's not now. I don't know whose house it is now, but it's not mine and it's not yours. Somewhere along the line we lost it. We're just . . . renting it, or something."

Nettie understood everything in that moment, so much so that she leaned her head back and nodded with gratitude to his honesty. She was able to picture what the house must look like to him, because it looked the same way to her. The only difference was that she watched it happen, as it happened. It all made sense to her now.

Ethan leaned forward, resting his elbows on his knees. "I want to leave eventually. Of course I do. But every time I start to psyche myself up, it's just . . ."

"I get it," she said. And when he looked into her eyes, she made sure he saw a mother who *did* get it, who *was* sympathetic and empathetic, or whatever. That felt important to her right now. After a few seconds, she puffed out her cheeks thoughtfully and looked around while he pretended to enjoy the spaghetti.

Nettie was hit with sudden inspiration. "Hey, you wanna do something for me?"

"Yeah sure," he said, mouth full of food.

"Can you look up the church in Spain?"

"The church in Spain," he said bluntly.

"The big one. The one in Barcelona."

He put down his plate and typed "Barcelona church" into Google.

"This says Sagrada Familia?"

Nettie jumped off of the couch and leaned over his shoulder as he clicked on a photo and zoomed in on it. It was the weirdest, ugliest thing she'd ever seen. The towers looked like symmetrical dirt dauber nests, or weird instruments, and the whole thing jutted upward like a patch of weeds. She couldn't imagine anyone looking at it and weeping. It was an unfinished, hideous mess. She had to assume it was prettier on the inside.

"What if we got you some medicine?" she said.

"What kind of medicine?" he asked nervously.

"Nothing weird. Just, I don't know. Medicine for anxiety."

"Don't you need a doctor for that?"

Nettie chewed on the inside of her lip absently. "Maybe not. I might be able to rustle up some."

"Jesus."

"Hey, you let me worry about it. I'm your mama. I'll figure something out." She looked at him. "We're not gonna be able to fix this today, or next week. But we're closer to fixing it now than we were an hour ago, right? There's a great big shitty world out there waiting for you." She thought about buttresses literally holding up the walls of cathedrals so they wouldn't collapse. "And you know what? I don't have what I used to have but I'm glad I have you, kid."

It wasn't something she planned on saying, and she almost regretted it when she saw Earl's green eyes staring up at her like she had spoken Japanese. Their family never made a habit of saying things like that. She could see his thinning face, foreign to her, bathed in the blue of the Barcelona skyline on the screen.

His expression suddenly softened. "I'm glad I have you, too."

She squeezed his shoulder and leaned down to watch him play for a few minutes. There was a chat box up on one side of the screen, reminding her of the chat room of the forum for lost parents. It was crawling with words of encouragement for GoatsinCoats and questions and smiling yellow faces and other signs of life. On the screen, Ethan was steering a woman in a metal suit with a giant gun on one arm, fighting monsters and demons that she knew would keep attacking her over and over again until the game was finally over.

STILL WATERS

DOWNHILL. THAT WAS THE WORD she used with Sergeant Simmons to describe the direction her husband had gone since his best friend overdosed.

Downhill. He had gone *downhill*.

"Do you think we should put him on administrative leave?" Simmons asked.

"That's probably best. You just didn't hear it from me."

"Oh, no, honey. Never. Do you feel okay?"

People-watching was the key to assimilating, she'd found, and assimilating was the closest thing to happiness Charlie could hope for. She wanted to remember what it felt like to sit in Austin's Grill with her husband instead of sitting alone, so she ate her hot dog and watched the others instead; Mitchell and Dora Canter were sitting with Johnny and Samantha Barnes, and Austin was calling people "Beau" and "Baby" and passing paper bags over the counter, and the slick fly paper wasn't working, and Susan was still trying to get people to go to prayer aerobics at her house. The men from the agricultural supply store came in a big herd, their blue collars collecting the brown sweat from the backs of their necks, hands leaving casual black smudges everywhere—an itchy nose or forehead, the light switch in the bathroom, the doorknobs, the steering wheels, everything. Hatcher's raggedy-muffin little kid was walking around looking for free food, and all of this was normal, as opposed to her house, which was not normal at all.

Someone in the kitchen slammed an oven door and she nearly jumped out of her skin.

"Charlie?"

"Hmm?"

"I asked if you felt okay being at the house with him."

"What do you mean?"

Simmons looked her dead in the eye. "Do you feel safe with him?"

It hadn't occurred to her that this was a thing she should even be worried about, so she nodded confidently and said, "Yeah, of course."

Later, Charlie stared out the kitchen window, watching Dale tinkering frantically on his truck as he listened to a podcast about the Holocaust. Knowing him lately, he was probably breaking something just so he could fix it again, over and over, like he was trying to exist between destruction and restoration at the same time. He used to chase her around with little bursts from the can of WD-40 while she laughed and swatted at him, dancing in her bare feet over their gravel driveway.

She pinned a towel beneath her chin and folded it numbly, watching him like she'd watch any stranger who had wandered into her yard—with confusion, caution, and a vague desire to call for help.

"The Holocaust is sort of morbid, isn't it?" she asked when

he came inside.

"It's history," he'd said firmly. "And it's interesting."

Her father told her once that meanness don't just happen overnight. Dale used to pass the time on his shifts by listening to late-night talk-radio shows in his car, which left the other passengers (doped-up kids and drunk people he had to take home and gently reprimand) no choice but to listen to the droning discussions on the curious extinction of the honeybees.

But now he had his own burgundy childhood *World Book Encyclopedia*, fished out of a box in the attic and cracked open on the passenger's seat to a page about the various types of executions throughout history.

Dale had been like a strong oak, suddenly tied down to grow crooked.

"When did his symptoms start?"

What a question.

Recently, she walked in to find him writing the words "I am not" on a piece of paper over and over again with a Sharpie, pressing down so hard that it started to stain the wood underneath. I am not, I am not, I am not.

"I am not what?" she'd asked, as gently as she could.

He scoffed, disgusted, and said, "Don't worry about it."

"I do worry," she answered. "I'll always worry about you."

"Don't."

But in this instance he'd seemed oddly impressed with himself, like this was a three-second wrestling match and he'd come out on top with her arm bent backward and nowhere to go. He enjoyed her concern. He enjoyed her fretting. Mostly she felt like a lottery ticket, her shining surface scratched and torn by her husband, desperate to see if he had won anything valuable in any given conversation. She longed for the smallest amount of genuine affection and intimacy, daydreaming about the faceless person who adjusted her seatbelt on the roller coaster, the dentist when he checked her throat for tumors, the bouncer in the city who wrapped the paper bracelet around her wrist, smiling and telling her to have a great time. It was amazing how much she missed the touch of another human.

There was a sign on Turnip Road in memory of Gentry Coats. Apparently, the whole road was dedicated in his memory—odd as that sounded when she really thought about it—and a few members of the town rotated to keep it clean of cigarette butts and beer bottles. They said Gentry's mother Nettie hadn't driven the road since they put the sign up, not until recently, when she was spotted like an elusive albino deer at the church where Gentry's funeral had been held.

The kudzu had already taken over the silver post of the sign. No one had bothered to clean it off for a while, because they knew it would just swarm it again in a week or so. Why bother? Why bother.

Charlie, Gentry, and Dale had grown up together, teasing each other with tobacco sticks and washed-up river trash— once even a doll with all its limbs pulled off. Then, one day as a teenager, Charlie suddenly noticed the white button-up shirt cuffed against Dale's tanned forearm in the church parking lot after the morning service, and she was done for. After that, she always made sure she was standing next to him in Sunday School so she could feel his big hand closing around hers when they stood and prayed. That was the first time she felt attracted to a praying man. Not a man who prays, but the sight of a man on one knee.

Dale didn't pray anymore.

—

Somewhere during all of this, Charlie stood beneath and looked up into Dale's family tree, examined its branches and fruit based on the stories she'd heard over the years, and noticed an eccentric thread stretching through the male side of things. His father had literally screamed himself to death, locked in the bedroom in what Simmons had called a *psychotic episode*. That was Charlie's first indicator that something wasn't quite right with the entire family, frankly.

They did not talk about it, especially not now. Recently, Dale's mother brought her dead husband up casually and Dale had shot her a glare that would've gotten him smacked had he been under eighteen.

Dale's grandfather's name was Amos, and he was crazy. Apparently, he didn't even really have Alzheimer's or delirium or any other crazy-inducing condition that was associated with old age—although Dale's mother would certainly tell you that Amos was nine days older than dirt. He was simply crazy. He'd been crazy since the day Dale was born, and had always been crazy to their knowledge, and would probably be crazy until the day he died, if he wasn't dead already. No one had seen him in over a decade.

Years ago, he could usually be found peddling bruised apples and berries and jerky at a roadside stand in the mountains. Charlie had only met him a handful of times throughout their childhood, but even she remembered that Amos was always obsessed with fruit. There was one for every disease, every ailment, and not just oranges for colds; papayas cured a stomachache; peaches cured constipation; bananas stopped diarrhea in babies; and three bites of a good, crisp apple would ease a headache instantly.

When Dale turned fifteen, his uncle (who put forth a half-hearted effort to be a paternal figure after his dad's death) gave him thirty dollars out of his wallet and said, "Go nuts, Boss." His mother went to the department store and bought Dale his first athletic cup so he could try out (unsuccessfully) for the football team. His grandmother, fifteen years divorced from Amos, bought him a bottle of cologne from the pharmacy.

But on the way to see them, Amos had spied a perfectly good *Sesame Street* kite peeking out of a garbage can at the top of someone's driveway. He presented it to Dale with great ceremony, insisting that he abandon his party so the two of them could go into the soybean field behind his house to fly it.

And you best believe Dale did it. He was the golden boy, even then, cherished by the entire town for his politeness, his eagerness to help people, his willingness to sit at the Table of Knowledge at the front of Austin's and actually listen to the old men telling their tales and talking politics and conspiracy theories. Dale was the person you'd call when you got drunk at the bar and needed a ride home, or when you ran off the road at three in the morning.

It's very hard to be with a flawless person. Charlie was so proud of Dale, but there was a darker part of her—a much darker part—that noticed he recently started legitimately enjoying the adoration, much as he never asked for it.

She now lived in a constant suspension between "look after yourself first" and that old classic "stand by your man." Because, yes, he was a good man and good things take time. If she stayed put for another year and a half, maybe she'd figure out how to tell the difference between what was worth waiting for and what would slip from her fingers if she didn't act now, now, now.

Her favorite hymn was the "Hymn of Promise," written by Natalie A. Sleeth in 1986. Now there was a bitch who knew that patience is a virtue, and that a watched pot doesn't boil until God says so.

They got along the majority of the time, until they tried to talk to one another, and that's usually when things started to go downhill. He apparently had the same idea about limiting the amount of interaction with her as she did with him, because when she timidly suggested they go on a date, he declared that he wanted to go to a movie, a place where they could face the same direction, untouching and unspeaking.

It was either that or nothing, she realized, and agreed.

Beforehand, Charlie flipped through her small collection of *Cosmopolitan* and *Woman's Day* magazines, reading articles about things like "Getting the Spark Back" and "Lighting his Fire Again." Taking her cue from one entitled "Who Says Flirting Has to Stop After Marriage?" she decided on a dangerous whim to send him a text message: *Hey hun, can't wait for our date tonight! :)*

Then, she waited for a response that never came. By two in the afternoon, her skin was flushed with embarrassment, and she kept slapping her forehead to try and forget she'd done it. By four, she'd considered just not bringing it up, ever. By six, she knew she'd have to straight-up apologize to avoid being mocked for it.

She waited until about an hour before he was due back from work to dig around in her makeup bag, until she found a tube of red lipstick that she hadn't used since their wedding a year and a half ago. When she took the cap off, she saw that it had somehow screwed itself up too far, and the lid had crushed the waxy tip into a paste. This forced her to use her finger to wipe some of it off and drag it across her mouth. It somehow felt dry and goopy at the same time, but it looked okay.

She was standing in the bathroom mirror with a curling iron in her hand when he walked in, way too early. She'd hoped to already be dressed and ready by the time he got home.

"Did you get my text?" she asked, somehow both exhilarated by and numbed at the idea of spending an evening with this man.

"Yeah." He sat on the bed with all of his gear still on and stared off at the other side of the room.

"Oh. You didn't respond, so I didn't know," she said, trying to keep her voice delicate and casual.

"I didn't know what you expected me to say to something like that."

"Anything," she answered, following his gaze to the dresser. "Just so I know you saw it."

In her general state of anxiety, she'd lost some of her gumption for doing basic household chores; all of their clothes were stacked haphazardly on top of the dresser, instead of tucked down where they were supposed to be.

"You know," he began, as casually as if he were about to discuss the weather. "This whole thing you've got going on—" he gestured to her vaguely and stood up "—you know, I can't figure out if I still want to be with you if you act like the apocalypse could happen at any moment, right?"

Charlie felt her heart drop to her stomach and her stomach leap into her throat. "If you still want to *be* with me!? When did *that* happen?"

"When you stopped acting like yourself."

"I stopped acting like myself when you stopped acting like yourself!" Hatred stiffened her spine.

"Then maybe you should consider acting natural."

"That's a real strange thing to do, Dale, putting a gun to someone's head and telling them to act natural."

He stared at the piles of clothes for a few more seconds, and without warning, swung his big arm out and knocked the stacks of shirts and pants and everything else off the dresser with one long, fast, fluid motion. Picture frames and belt buckles and little bowls with earrings and dimes and nickels clattered to the carpet. Dale gave a shuddering growl that barely sounded human, then suddenly looked at her with mild horror as she stood there, trembling at his rage, with her eyes wide and pupils dilated in fear.

There was a beat of deep, frightening silence, the silence just beyond the line that was never meant to be crossed.

"I'm sorry," he said, looking at the clothes on the floor, almost as if he were apologizing to them and not her.

"It's okay," she answered instinctively, with a slight stutter from her shaking. Her desire to keep him from getting more upset felt more overwhelming to her than her own fear and anger.

They didn't make it to the movie, but after an hour or two of the cold-shoulder orbit around the house, they did go ahead and have make-up sex that felt irreverent and awkward, timid and warm, familiar and cold. Their sadness and fear came together and doubled.

That night she woke up to find him sitting on the edge of the bed, staring into the white noise between his fists as they rested on his knees, into the place where dark and light aren't separate. He seemed to find only bits and pieces of anything in the droning on and on in his head.

Angry and scared as she was of him, Charlie laid awake

and imagined the grief and confusion of an entire hive of disappearing honeybees humming in his stomach, and she desperately wanted to summon the compassion she'd need to weep for him.

Dale told her a story once. He was eight years old, and got up early one morning to get a glass of water. He rounded the corner of the hallway and startled his father, who had gotten up to pee. Both of them gasped, and his Dad's big hand shot out and slapped Dale so hard that his head twisted, sending him flying into the opposite wall. The pain readied Dale instantly for a fight. He balled his fists and flew back to his feet only to see that his father's hands were covering his mouth, tears in his eyes, looking horrified, like he'd seen a ghost, or some part of himself that he'd been praying for a long time was not there. Charlie figured it must have been like that moment when you first say something that sounds exactly like something your mother would say, only not quite.

With each new and frightening incident over the following weeks, the edges of Charlie's nerves slowly ripped into tattered threads. She felt like some small, pitiful rodent in a hole, it's life forced to revolve around the habits and movements of a nearby snake. Before long, she had learned to tell what kind of mood Dale was in by the types of sounds she heard emanating from the garage at night, how hunched his spine was as he sat on the edge of the bed staring at the carpet, how many hours he spent in the living room with the TV on to cover the sound of him talking to himself, how much food he ate, or didn't, how many swallows of vodka he took straight from the dust-covered bottle in the cabinet above their stove just before bed, and most importantly, by the way he came down the driveway and climbed out of his patrol car at night.

This one dictated so much of her evening that she felt completely lost to the wind if she missed the opportunity to observe it firsthand. If Dale pulled into the driveway at about thirty-five before sitting in his car for a few minutes playing on his phone, things were going to be fine… provided he then closed the door normally and skipped three of the five stairs on the porch. If all those conditions were in place, it meant they were going to have an okay evening—maybe even sort of *normal*, whatever *normal* was these days. But if he pulled slowly into the driveway, got out the car immediately, and placed a deliberate, condemning boot on each and every step of the porch stairs, it was going to be bad. Very bad.

The bugs were deafeningly loud, tonight. It had rained too much this year, and the tobacco fields around the road were different shades of emerald, dark green and ranked up. Charlie stood on the porch in her bare feet, smoking a cigarette—a habit she'd only picked back up in the last few weeks, either a cry of rebellion or a cry for help, and watched the clock on her cell phone ticking up to six o'clock like a bomb counting down to zero.

She thought about Amos, again. Dale's grandfather had been homeless since the day he was kicked out after the divorce. He lived in a trailer he pulled behind a puttering white van, full of boxes and crates of rotten fruit purchased wholesale from farmers markets in Florida, Georgia, and South Carolina. He stopped by to see his family whenever his wanderings allowed, but it wasn't something people looked forward to. *Crazy* was not something people wanted in this town. Not even the honeybees wanted anything to do with him.

When she was a kid, she spent most of her summers

wandering around town with Dale and Gentry. She thought Amos was fun enough, until he offered to pay Charlie and Dale ten dollars to clean out his enclosed trailer full of sweet potatoes that had been baking in the sun for about two months. A swarm of maggots had been hiding under a box, squirming in and out of the rotten skins like they were feeding on dead rats. A few of them already had wings and dispersed into Charlie and Dale's faces, and she ran outside and threw up into the grass until she dry heaved. Amos gave them both five dollars. The next day, Dale said he watched from the living room while his mother and Amos argued on the back porch.

"Just get your nasty shit out of my yard before I put a match to it," Mary said, her voice low and rumbling in a way that was ten times more terrifying than yelling.

It seemed mean at the time, but it was before Charlie came to learn that irrevocable hatred has a bad reputation. It's a special kind of fire, the kind you can learn to harness and use for warmth and fuel when someone lets you down or disgusts you.

Dale and Mary Overton had come home from church that afternoon to find no less than fifteen bruised watermelons floating in their above-ground pool, bobbing in the warm chlorine water. Mary calmly told Dale to go get on his bathing suit and fish them out, which he took for some kind of game. Amos disappeared after that.

"Crazy bastard," Mary would say of him, even now. And not the good kind of crazy.

Waiting for her husband to come home, Charlie wondered how many wives had sat in their armchairs, or stood on their porches anxiously cleaning the dirt out from under their fingernails with the sharp points of their necklaces, waiting for the noises that would determine the rest of their night . . . waiting with bated breath to see what mood a man was in, just because the man was crazy enough to dictate their entire lives. How many women had done what she's doing now?

But giving craziness a gender might be unfair. Charlie's own grandmother Rosa was also said to have been crazy. Charlie didn't remember her, so she couldn't say for sure, but the few stories she'd heard were of a woman afflicted with wildness and an inability to conform to anything. Rosa's husband was not crazy, but in the seventies had purchased a how-to book on housekeeping for Rosa on the occasion of their thirtieth anniversary. The story goes that she let out a battle cry in the middle of the Golden Corral, hurled the book across the room at his face in front of the entire family, and didn't cook, clean, do laundry or wash dishes for a month. Her crowning moment, however, was a few weeks after she turned eighty-nine and a few months before she died, when one of her grandchildren pulled into the driveway and caught her hanging laundry in the backyard wearing nothing but a white bra and a pair of yellow cotton panties. This was not Alzheimer's or elderly delirium either. It was simply Rosa. When questioned about her attire, she said the words that would live in infamy, so famous among her loved ones and so telling of her personality that Charlie was surprised someone didn't include it in her epitaph:

"What? From the road, it looks just like a bathing suit."

Charlie went through a particularly stubborn phase as a child where she insisted on wearing one of her father's wife-beaters, a hot pink tutu from Goodwill and a cowboy hat everywhere she went. At one point, her mother shook her head, leaned in, and whispered an almost biblical warning to her father: "The spirit of Rosa is in that child." Her mother, knowing the genetics of her in-laws, went to Penny's the very next day to buy Charlie a khaki skirt that she wore once and a starched white blouse that she buried almost immediately under the pink, itchy insulation in their attic in the hopes that it would rot into maggot food.

Charlie would never say it out loud, but Rosa's brand of craziness was admirable to her, powerful and feminine. Anyone would be lucky to have it.

She lifted her head and quickly extinguished her cigarette on the porch rail when she saw the patrol car coming down the street. It practically came to a stop at the entrance of the driveway, then slowly turned in. Too slowly. Dale climbed out of the car immediately once it was turned off and briefly jerked his chin up by way of a greeting. Then he went inside without a word, taking each and every step on the way, and going straight upstairs to change.

Fuck.

She was standing over the stove anxiously making spaghetti when he finally came down to sit at the kitchen table. Charlie remembered what he'd said about acting natural and tried to relax her posture, but she couldn't stop the wave of resentment and hatred that slammed into her when she did it.

"They've put me on administrative leave," he announced.

Charlie was quiet for a moment, using the spatula to push the hissing peppers and onions and beef around to try to burn off all the grease. "Why?" she finally asked, hoping to God she could effectively pretend she had nothing to do with it. .

"They think I'm *mentally and emotionally unfit.*"

She glanced over her shoulder at him. He was sitting square to her, leaned back in the chair, legs crossed like a mob boss during an interrogation in a movie. Orange was the color she would remember the most about that night, especially his narrowed eyes in the dim amber of the ancient bulb in the ancient fixture above their dinner table. He was looking at her like she was an enemy. He didn't even look at criminals that way. He had never looked at anyone that way.

"Well at least it's administrative leave and not, you know. Real leave-leave."

"It's unfair."

She turned back to the food and plucked a noodle from the hot water to see how soft it had gotten. "It's ready."

"Don't you think it's unfair?"

"Plate or bowl?"

"Charlotte."

"I . . . think it's fair."

He stood up so fast his chair screeched out behind him. It made her jump, and that's when she began to shake. Dale slowly walked across the kitchen and slammed a cabinet open nearly hard enough to break it, getting himself a plate.

"Why do you think it's fair?" he asked, scooping his noodles out with a feigned calmness.

Charlie backed out of his way and went to sit. "You seem angry lately."

"You're not having any?"

"I'm not hungry. I will later."

"Are you pregnant or something?"

She wrinkled her nose in disgust. "No, I'm not fucking pregnant."

"When did we stop trying?" he asked, sitting down, not taking his glowing orange eyes off of her.

"When you got so . . . *angry.*"

He scoffed loudly "I'm angry because everyone seems to

think I'm some kind of monster! You know, I *could* be a monster. I *could* kick your ass right now if I wanted. Then I'd *really* be a monster. But I won't."

There was a little muscle, just to the right of her mouth, that twitched so violently she just knew it had to be visible. Her body was telling her that it was time.

"You're acting crazy," she said. "You're acting just like your dad."

He set his jaw and launched his hand, quick as an angry dog, toward his plate. Charlie ducked down, tornado-style, hands laced on top of her head with a clipped scream. The plate shattered on the wall behind her, raining ceramic shards and boiling hot pasta down on her. She yelped and jerked to her feet so hard that the chair flew back to crack the door of the china cabinet.

Charlie whimpered and slapped at her skin to get the hot noodles and sauce off of her, then sat there for a moment, eyes frozen in place on the long-abandoned ovulation calendar on the refrigerator.

"Get out," she growled, with a power she had not felt until now. Her fight-or-flight instincts had kicked in, her hatred making her as vicious as a lion. Her daddy always said that letting the cat out of the bag is a lot easier than putting it back in, and she felt changed in that moment. "Get out and get help."

"You're acting crazy," he said.

"You're acting *fucking* crazy!" she answered, shaking with the pain of the burns, with indignation, with fear. "Get out and get help!"

He took his glass of tea and hurled it against the wall, but now he seemed more like a child having a tantrum. He thought she was fucking around, that he could scare her out of the decision. She wasn't fucking around. There had been vows, rings disintegrating in front of her face, solids turned to liquids, liquids to steam, steam curling up into the sky and turning into nothing, making her wonder if those promises had ever been there to begin with. To have and to hold, for richer and for poorer, in sickness and in health. As long as we both shall live.

"I just want you to get help, Dale," she said as he walked out, trying to be gentle.

"I want you to go straight to Hell."

Those were the last words her husband spoke to her before he left. Charlie stood on the porch hugging herself as he spun tires out of the driveway. The moon cast a skeleton shadow through the single tree in their yard, stretching from the cracked earth like a thirsty cry for help. Whoever had recently moved in next door had swept away the grass clippings, because while she couldn't see that the yard had been recently mowed, she could smell it, the sliced blades casting the bitter scent of life after death all down the street.

In the days that followed, Charlie's state of mind sank quickly until she completely submerged herself in loneliness, and not an okay loneliness, either—not at all like that sad song on the radio that somehow makes you feel better—but like when you go to the grocery store and see people you know and you'd much rather just go straight back home and slam the door in the world's face rather than say hello.

So she slowly peeled off her responsibilities, like Sunday school and weekly lunches with friends and returning Dale's mothers' fifteen phone calls, and threw them down like shattering glass, promising herself that she'd clean them up later, like the glass of the china cabinet that still littered the kitchen floor.

At this point, it was hard to believe she'd ever wanted kids with him. Now the idea of children in general was revolting and impractical, like planting flowers in bad dirt. They would never know anything, and eventually, whatever child she had would have a child, and that child wouldn't know anything either. And maybe those kids would have kids who would never know anything, and grandchildren who would never know anything, and grandchildren who would never know anything.

In some ways that shattered plate was exactly what she had needed.

She would not remember much about the day she moved out, only that it happened very fast, nails jutting crooked from the mantle where their stockings used to hang all year, the emptiness of a room with exactly half of the furniture snatched out of it, great imprints in the carpet next to Kool-Aid and coffee stains.

When she turned and took a final look, the little brick house seemed like a good sneeze could knock it right down.

But she would go on to have nightmares about it, several times a week. Sometimes she was trapped inside alone, and the walls were burning. Sometimes she was outside and the walls were burning, but Dale was inside, and she couldn't find a way in to help him. She dreamt that she was walking through the house stepping over dozens of partially decomposed bodies, their green leathery skin pulled tight and stuck like an Edvard Munch painting. She would see herself forced inside by a tornado ripping through the field. She would hide behind the couch from soldiers looking for her. She would cower from a great noise shaking the walls down, and she would fold up in silent agony like a dying spider at the sight of a red pulsing glow coming from the light fixtures.

Charlie knew about the mysterious disappearance of the honeybees. Was it radiation poisoning? Toxicity from pollution? Outright extinction? Maybe the answer was on the radio in the waiting room, where her husband was waiting to be taken upstairs.

TRESPASSES

Officer Dale Overton was in the recreation room writing about the death penalty in crayon when Sarah Hatcher walked in with a menu, a caddy of needles and vials, and those giant blue rubber bands that snapped on his skin and pinched his upper arm. His hospital gown was mint green and his crayon was robin's-egg blue. He was making a bulleted list as facts came to him in little bursts:

—*new york built first electric chair, 1888*
—*"more humane" than hanging or firing squad*
—*black mask protected dignity of victim*
—*also to keep eyeballs from falling out*

Finding information in his mind was like trying to find the Pleiades in the sky; he couldn't look at a concept straight on without losing it. Dale had to approach everything from the side, from phrases and images and seemingly unrelated words. The list was crooked on the paper, tilting more and more left with every line.

Sarah Hatcher glanced over his shoulder as she counted out

the plastic vials.

"You writing something?" she asked, obviously trying to be friendly. He hid the papers with his arm and glared.

Dale imagined suffocating on his own breath inside a burlap bag and decided he would want to die breathing freely. This made him think of the thick plastic windows here in the ward, and the bolts holding them shut. He'd give anything for one that opened, just a crack, to let in the bite of the autumn air that he had not felt after spending fifteen hours in the emergency room and who knew how many in the ward. He was starting to obsess over the electric yellow of the sun the same way a person can't think of anything but their toes when their shoes are too tight.

He'd shut himself up in his room yesterday and pressed his unshaved cheek against the warm plastic to watch the parking lot for the pickup truck. He counted the windows on the next building to figure out that he was on the fifth floor.

His nurse used to babysit him as a child in Bethany, before her two girls were born, and now she was assigned to check his lithium levels every day. He'd seen her sitting next to Gentry's mother, Nettie, just last Sunday. Being married to Jackson Hatcher and having two daughters with him had given her thin wrists, fat arms, giant hands, and a face that seemed forever pulled into an expression of mild terror. She was shaped vaguely like Gumby. "Can I get at your arm, Dale?"

"My name is Officer Overton," he announced, irritated.

"Officer Overton?" she said, meekly.

Dale pushed up his sleeve and dropped his forearm on the table. Sarah accidentally snapped the tourniquet around his arm, just like he knew she would, and apologized. She was chewing spearmint-flavored gum. He could smell it. He could smell everything—the alcohol swab, the latex on her gloves, the rubber on the band, his own breath, the crayon on the table.

"What can I get you to eat?" she asked, prepping the needle.

He snatched the menu from the table in front of her. He had to fill it out for the next day's meals every day, as though he could predict what he would be in the mood to eat an entire twenty-four hours in advance. For each meal, he could have one main dish, two sides, one type of bread, two different drinks, and one dessert. It was surprisingly extensive, four pages long, with everything from bourbon chicken to beef curry to cheesesteaks and burgers. Grams of sugar were listed in a column next to each item on the list. Last night, a gigantic woman with nubs for legs ate two hot dogs, an eggroll, garlic bread, chips, and salsa. When the nurses turned their backs, she hurried to dump two packs of sugar into her pudding, then grinned at Dale as if she had just robbed a bank.

He looked away from the needle and kept shuffling for facts in his mind to distract himself from the little bite of pain he knew was coming.

—*first the prisoner is asked for final words*
—*sack placed on head*
—*silent signal given by warden to man in charge of pulling the lever*

His best friend Gentry had talked him into riding "The Plunge" at the state fair when they were fifteen. It was a giant tower that took a ring of about thirty riders over three hundred feet into the air before dropping them straight down. Dale didn't mind the drop as much as he minded not knowing when the drop would happen, being up there, suspended, gripping the handlebars, too nervous to enjoy the spectacular view. When would it come? Now? How about . . . *now?* Could a prisoner ask for a countdown from five? Ten? Sixty? Would he want one? Would it be better to not know? What would he do with that final second even if he knew which one it was?

Here we go, Gentry laughed. *Hold on to your socks.*

The needle pushed into his vein, and Sarah clicked a vial into place on the port.

"You gonna donate all this blood to Red Cross when you're done with it, Dracula?" He rattled the laminated menu noisily in her face, causing her to flinch like it had hit her. "There's no white trash food on here. I guess you must fucking starve." It wasn't something he would've said to her six months ago. Hell, it wasn't something he would've *thought* six months ago.

"The Mexican is good," she said. He looked away when she pulled the rubber band loose and felt his blood rushing through the tube. It looked black.

"I've already had the burrito," he said.

"It's really good." Sarah slid the needle out from beneath a wad of gauze, and he pressed his left palm against it without needing to be asked. The back of his hand erupted with tremors and jumps that got worse when he was under any kind of stress. That's what finally made Sergeant Simmons force him into medical leave—not his constant yelling into the radio and at kids, or the hours of parking he did on back roads, or the paranoid speeches at the station about how they all needed to be ready for the insurance fire being concocted by the knitting group that met in the basement of the Methodist church once a week. No, it was the shaking, surely.

Real cops don't shake.

Without his job in law enforcement, which was the only sense of purpose he'd ever had, all he could do was scream at his wife and ignore his mother's phone calls and have nightmares about his father and hear his dead best friend's voice at inappropriate moments . . . and get sent to psyche wards, apparently.

"Will Charlotte be visiting you tonight?" Sarah asked hopefully, writing "D. Overton" on the vials. "She would know how to cheer you up."

The last time he'd seen his wife, he had thrown a plate of spaghetti at her. Not at the wall. Not in her general direction. *At* her. Yet he couldn't seem to conjure up any guilt, especially when the very next memory he had was of her screaming at him to go and not to come back until he'd gotten help. There had been sauce on her chest, staining her shirt. She was fed up.

You're just like your father, Gentry said. *But who says that's a bad thing?*

"Your mama, maybe?" Sarah said softly. "I could give her a call for you?"

"She thinks I'm going to make the baby sick."

"Your mama?"

"No. Charlie." He circled the burrito, chips and salsa, rice, refried beans, an orange Gatorade, a bottle of water, and chocolate pudding. "I know she's afraid any baby we have is going to be crazy like me."

"Crazy isn't a word we like to use around here."

"Like I give a shit."

"Would you like for me to ask for one of our counselors to come see you? It'll be good to talk. It'll ease your mind about some of this."

"Fuck off."

Sarah taped the cotton to Dale's arm. "Well, let us know if you need anything."

"Fuck off, I said."

She picked up her caddy, and went back out into the

common area of geriatric psyche. There hadn't been a bed available in the general ward, but he liked that the demented elderly patients were so detached from reality that they didn't notice him. He didn't need to learn their names, or speak to them, or bump into them in the hallways. He didn't need to lash out at anyone as long as they all left him alone. He desperately needed to be alone.

Dale grabbed his blue crayon again.

—*two shocks*

—*first, 3,000-4,000 volts, renders the victim brain-dead*

—*the other, much smaller, fries the organs*

—*first shock can kill a person quicker than a pain signal, fraction of a second*

—*after lethal injections, electrocutions most botched form of execution*

Willie Francis survived his first trip to the electric chair, and all he said about the experience was that it made his mouth taste like cold peanut butter. Ol' Willie didn't get a pass for cheating death. He was executed properly a week later.

—*two nodes create current*

—*attached at the top of the head and around inmate's ankle*

—*sponge soaked in salt water must be real sea sponge, fake ones catch on f—*

The crayon snapped in his shaking fist. He tossed it into the growing pile of wax crumbs too small even to pinch between his thumb and forefinger.

Dale could deal with the irritability and paranoia. He even liked that Gentry had never really left him. He could deal with all of that if it weren't for the physical feeling. Nothing could distract him from it. It kept him awake for days at a time—restless, heavy, and moving like a snake through his stomach and chest and back down, slithering through his intestines before coiling up in his stomach again. The snake was the reason he shook. It was the reason he'd gone from a calm, reasonable officer of the law to a man who couldn't even order lunch without insulting someone. It made him bang on the locked door of the "psychiatric evaluation room" in the emergency department when he first arrived, like some kind of drug addict, which was exactly what they thought he was—strung out on cocaine, or pills, or heroin like Gentry had been. Dale had been hearing Gentry's voice ever since the day he died, first a short outburst here or there, but then more frequent, until it was hard *not* to engage it in conversation.

When his piss came back clean, a nurse came into the padded room said, "So, this does look like a kind of psychosis. You definitely did the right thing by coming here. Does your family have a history of—"

"Fuck off."

Your dad doesn't have anything to do with this, Gentry said. *What a bitch.*

Dale reached for a crayon that was light purple, lavender like his mother's Easter dress.

—shitting and pissing normal during execution
—cotton inserted into rectum

Dale was starting on gas chambers when Sarah came over the intercom and announced "Group in ten minutes." The old people groaned to their feet, if they had feet, and began wobbling and shuffling and rolling toward the recreation room where he was sitting.

Once, a death-row inmate in Missouri who, when given the choice between lethal injection, gas, or electrocution, opted for the long-unused gas chamber with its full minutes of suffering that probably felt more like hours simply because it was the most expensive, required the most effort, and was the most dangerous for the execution team to operate.

If you have to die, at least be an inconvenience, Gentry said.

Dale elbowed his way to the front desk. A small white board on the wall had a hand-drawn calendar on it no one had updated in weeks. There was no time in this place. He had no idea how long he'd been here.

"I just wanted to let you know that I'm not going to group today," he said.

The nurse didn't look up from her computer. Her name was Shanice. Shanice had curly black hair pulled into a bun that made her about six inches taller than she would've been otherwise. "Group is required for all patients," she said.

There was a half-dead man named Mr. Louis in an armchair in the common room. Dale had never seen him move. Every few hours, the nurses leaned his armchair back, changed his diaper in front of everyone, put his gown back down, and sat him back up so he could stare blankly at the wall for four hours until they did it again. His face looked like it was already decomposing.

"Okay. If that man goes," he pointed. "Then I'll go."

"Mr. Louis has a customized care plan."

"He sits in a chair and shits on himself," Dale said, and Gentry laughed.

"I'm not at liberty to discuss Mr. Louis' care plan with you."

Is she going to come change your diaper if you shit yourself?

"Are you going to come change my diaper if I shit myself?"

Shanice popped her gum. "That's not in your care plan."

"I want his care plan, then. Where do I sign up?"

He wanted her to look at him. He wanted her to realize that he was not like the other people here. He was only here to appease his wife and his boss. He was fine. He wanted to grab the monitor and throw it at her. He wanted to reach for the gun he didn't have and fire it into the air, punctuating every shot with *look at me, look at me, look at me.*

She said, "You can discuss your plan with the doctor tomorrow morning."

"I need to go for a walk outside. Someone needs to unlock the door."

"Patients are not allowed to leave the ward until discharge."

"Why?" he asked. "Afraid someone might want to leave?"

She finally looked up. "Mr. Overton, is there something I can do for you?"

She needs to get hit for that fucking attitude, Gentry said.

"Don't fucking go there, man," Dale said to him, out loud.

Shanice raised an eyebrow and Sarah Hatcher—who was folding gowns behind the desk—looked up in alarm.

Dale said, "I'm an officer of the Bethany Police Department and I want everyone in this fucking ward to be treated the same. This is America. I don't want to go to group but I have to and he doesn't? What a joke. I'm a grown ass man. I don't want to go to a class on how to have Alzheimer's. I don't have Alzheimer's. Why should I waste my time? That's stupid. You'd have to be stupid to not see how stupid that is. It's fucking stupid."

Like you've got anything better to do, Gentry said.

"I told you to shut up," Dale said.

Shanice pulled a clipboard with his name on it from a rack beside her, not taking her eyes off of him. "You seem agitated, Mr. Overton. Would you like to take your anti-psychotic?"

—inmates instructed to breathe deeply once chemicals are active in the gas chamber

"Is that a threat?" Dale asked. "Are you threatening me?"

—this speeds up the death process

"I'm asking if taking your medication early today would make you more comfortable."

"Fuck you."

Dale went back to the recreation room and slammed himself into an empty chair. A blonde college kid doing her medical residency was already standing at the front of the room, holding up a small piece of plywood with a doorknob, a light switch, a chain lock, and a television dial all screwed to it. She was demonstrating the various tasks and talking to the patients about turning faucets on and off, opening doors, and putting silverware in drawers.

"These things are important for those of you who are trying to maintain your independence for as long as possible."

Little late for that, Gentry said.

"Would you shut up?" Dale said. A few people looked at him.

The snake in Dale's gut felt like it was trying to catch its own tail. He snatched a magazine about diabetes and used it as a makeshift desk on his lap, writing furiously. The med student cleared her throat and kept talking like he hadn't said anything.

—*a long stethoscope taped to the prisoner's chest leads to the outside of the chamber*

—*gas must be fully drained from chamber before body can be retrieved*

—*by far most dangerous execution method for crew*

—*can take fifteen minutes for inmate to die*

Back home, Charlie had a calendar on their refrigerator marked with happy faces for days when she was ovulating, faces with straight lines for mouths for days when she was not ovulating but could still get pregnant, and frowny faces for days when Dale didn't have to have sex with her. She was off her pills, but all of the sex stopped anyway once the snake came around. Not having sex made him angry, and not having sex the way he wanted made him angrier. Her telling him when he should and shouldn't have sex made him angrier still, and after a while, him being angry started making her angry. Dale's father had been an angry person too, before he died.

The med student moved her arms too much and had obviously spent time in the elevator memorizing a script before she came in. She was unnaturally regurgitating facts for no reason to a room that was not listening.

—*sodium cyanide dropped into a pail of sulfuric acid under the prisoner's chair*

—*sodium cyanide + sulfuric acid = hydrogen cyanide gas*

"When we feel icky, it can be hard to do simple things," she said. "But it's important that we do them every day, so we can remember how, right?"

Charlie once put her hand on the back of his neck and said "I can't wait for us to be parents." He used to be in love with the idea, too, but now he knew that there was no romance in it. He'd knock her up with some rug rat as fucked up as he was, she'd punch it out in a pile of snot and blood, and they'd spend the rest of their lives trying to convince themselves it didn't take after him.

The resident said something about not being ashamed to "ask loved ones for help if we need it" even when it's tempting to push people away, and Dale looked up.

"But what if you're *not* knocking on death's door?" he asked. A truly ancient old lady looked at him, shaking hands curled over sunken breasts that may have fed children in a past life. "What if you have something other than Alzheimer's? What if you're not supposed to be here at all?" He threw his crayon to the floor, breaking it. "When are we going to talk about me?"

The giant woman with nubs for legs clapped twice, smiling like she'd just seen a terrier jump through a hoop. Another patient said, "What? What's that? Speak up."

Dale stood up and slammed the door open with his shoulder to get back into the common area.

"Dale, honey," Sarah said as he walked past the desk. In this light, her eyes had a frightened, bruised look to them. "Officer Overton, I've asked your doctors to review a change on your dose tonight. I really hope it'll make you more comfortable. Please let me know if there's anything else I can do. Are you sure you don't want me to call your mom?"

"Just fuck off."

He tried to slam the door to his hospital room, but it was hydraulic and hissed helplessly in response before closing with a small click. At med call, there were four pills in his little plastic cup instead of two, and he had to open his mouth wide and lift his tongue for the nurse after he swallowed them.

That night, he dreamt about Charlie sitting at their kitchen table at home, naked and pregnant, with disgusting blue veins snaking across her stretched stomach. She had a brown leather strap under her chin and another one wrapped around her bony ankle. A small cap pressed a wet sponge against the top of her head as salt water streamed from her eyes and she was smiling at him and holding her belly and he was trying to calculate how many volts it would take to kill them both.

Someone knocked at five in the morning. The nurse from the desk yesterday morning, Shanice, told him not to get up. Dale's arm weighed three tons and he couldn't lift it into the blood pressure cuff.

"That's all right, honey," she said softly. "I've got you. You just keep resting."

The sterile white light coming into his dark room was too much. He closed his eyes.

"Your blood pressure is better," she said, tearing the velcro. "Do you feel better?"

Dale's head swam and his lungs rattled. He didn't understand the question. He waited for a voice to tell him what to do or what to say, but hers was the only one he heard. "Get some more rest, sweetheart."

Get the license plate of whatever hit you man, Gentry said, quietly.

Dale pushed at the mattress with his hands, then fell back again. He slept through breakfast and missed group and tried three times to get up and couldn't justify trying again. The death penalty lists and a few broken crayons laid on the nightstand. He reached for them but his hand shook and fell.

The doctors made their rounds at eleven, a man and a woman with blurry nametags.

"How are we feeling today, Mr. Overton?" the woman asked.

Why do doctors always talk about we? Gentry wondered.

Dale struggled to refocus his eyes, blinking.

She offered, "A little sedated, maybe? Mixed episodes with psychotic features go down hard. Totally normal."

Dale had plenty to say to them about normal, but saying it would take too much effort.

"Do you mind if we ask you a few questions?" she asked.

"You can just nod or shake," the male doctor added.

Dale nodded.

"Do you feel like others are out to harm you?" the woman doctor asked. "Do you feel paranoid about interpersonal relationships? Do you feel unnecessarily aggressive toward other people? Any homicidal thoughts or thoughts to harm yourself? Thoughts of death? Can you see or hear things that other people cannot see or hear? Do you find yourself speaking too quickly or repeating yourself? Any thoughts that life is not worth living?"

Dale nodded. Or maybe he shook.

"We're going to rein some things in tonight," the female doctor said. "See how you do tomorrow."

A few minutes later he had to stumble to the bathroom with diarrhea like battery acid. Then, a male nurse half-carried him to a table in the main room, where a blue plastic tray appeared in front of him—burrito, chips, salsa, rice, refried beans, an orange Gatorade, a bottle of water, and chocolate pudding.

He struggled to lift his plastic fork to take a bite of rice.

Most inmates request regular prison fare for their final meal, Gentry said. Or was it him? Dale was too confused to eat.

The woman in the wheelchair across from him asked if he wanted his pudding. Her nubs looked like the wrinkled ends of sausages, pinched to broken ends.

Dale shook his head.

She grabbed the small cup with a bloated hand. She didn't look as old as the others, and looked more swollen than obese, like a human water balloon about to burst.

"My name's Lucy," she said. "I seen you around."

Dale struggled to lift his eyes, his head a bowling ball on a toothpick.

"You mad as a hornet yesterday in group," she said. She had chocolate pudding on her chin. "Mad as a hornet."

Yesterday felt like years ago. Dale looked down at his food.

What the hell was he was thinking when he ordered this? How could it have possibly seemed appetizing?

He struggled to remember his wife's name.

Suddenly Lucy had tears in her eyes. "Doctors say I'm gonna die in a few weeks."

Dale stared at her.

Charlotte.

Lucy's face lit back up. She opened her mouth to reveal two brown teeth. "Woo-whee," she said. "That's good pudding!"

Charlie was peeing on a stick in their bathroom right now. He knew it. His stomach lurched and he stumbled back to his room. He threw his gown off and fell naked onto the toilet, holding on to the railing on the wall.

Hold on to your socks, Gentry said.

All the pollution and chemicals and meanness rushed out of him. He wanted to have diarrhea and vomit until he died. He wanted to go to wherever Gentry was, and his father, and never have to see another plate of spaghetti ever again.

—several minutes of saline before a lethal injection expands and lubricates the veins

Dale flushed the toilet and pushed himself to his feet. The mirror was dirty, splashes of thick white along the edges from bad paint jobs. He squinted, trying to see a father in his reflection before his eyes blurred again. Dale remembered the day his father died only in faint sensory details. The sudden silence from the bedroom, the sirens in the driveway, the antique mirror in the living room reflecting red and blue lights from outside along the walls, the yellow pages on the counter as his mother searched for the number of the funeral home, the way the brakes squeaked when the old black van pulled into the driveway, the cold taste of a banana popsicle in his mouth that his mother had given him when she told him to wait on the back porch, the beagle-themed calendar on the refrigerator, still showing April puppies in a bucket with daisies on their heads even though it was June.

The shower stall was yellow with a dirty-white light and no shower curtain. Someone could get hold of a hospital gown and take advantage of a metal bar. He'd never thought about suicide, in the sense that he felt his life was too agonizing and hopeless to live, but now he couldn't help but wonder if staying alive would be more difficult than just letting himself go.

It's like falling asleep, Gentry said. *It really is like falling asleep.*

—*"i've done 89 executions and only one of them fought, most are ready" said the warden of San Quentin*

The water blasted like a fire hose out of the faucet. It would only turn on for ten seconds at a time. Dale kept one hand on the silver button to support his weight and used the other to manage the travel-sized bottle of baby shampoo they'd given him to wash with. He considered asking someone for help but decided his last shred of dignity was more important.

Afterward Dale fell into bed, soaking wet. He covered himself with a fresh hospital gown like a blanket. It was yellow and scratchy, with the remnants of a vomit stain on the sleeve.

"Mr. Overton?" Dale opened his eyes an hour later. "You have a visitor."

Charlie, he thought instantly, a hopeful jerk in his stomach that he had not expected considering how mad at her he still was. He wiggled his still-naked body under the blanket, then groped to find the button that would lift the head of his bed.

But it was his mother he saw at the desk, handing her purse to the guard. His nurse, Sarah, came around the corner and hugged her with a long, meaningful squeeze that he realized was sympathy.

It wasn't until now that Dale *really* remembered how crucial Sarah had been to them when Dale's father died, long before her own girls were born. Sarah went to the grocery store for them, mowed the lawn a few times, and took Dale to school his entire fifth grade year on her way to work. She really was a patient, gentle woman. She'd have to be, to do the job she was doing, dealing with people like him. Jackson didn't deserve her. He called his wife "Woman" to her face and spat indoors and let their daughters play with his guns. Jackson was out of work and salty, the nastiest man in Bethany by far. Even at Dale's father's worst—and his worst was worse than most—he never treated anyone that way. Dale had a hard time remembering his father smiling or the sound of his voice when he wasn't yelling about something, but he didn't remember blatant cruelty.

Back when Dale was still in training, Jackson had jokingly said, "Now, you take it easy on me when you're a cop, boy." And Dale had. But looking at Sarah's sunken face today made him wonder if he needed to start checking in on their family more often, once he got his uniform back on, whenever that would be.

Dale closed his eyes when his mother walked in. He felt instantly overwhelmed by the presence of someone he really knew. She laid her hand on his forehead and tears streamed down his face. She sat on the edge of the bed.

"Hey," she said comfortingly. "Hey, hey. You're all right."

"Where's Charlie?" he asked.

"She's worried about you," she said.

"That's not what I asked."

"Medicine knock you on your ass?"

"Took it out of me, all right."

"That's what you needed," she said. She took her hand off his head and rested it on the blanket, on top of his stomach where the snake lay silent. "You threw spaghetti at her?"

"She was talking shit," he said, holding up his trembling hands as high as he could. "Told me I was getting to be like Dad."

His mother exhaled deeply and looked out of the window. In Charlie's defense, his father's hands did used to shake. Dale remembered him smashing a jelly jar on the floor of the kitchen when he couldn't get it open. Dale cut his foot weeks later on a tiny shard of glass that his mother had missed when she was cleaning up. She looked like she was remembering that too, or one of the hundreds of other times his father had snapped in rage then collapsed weeping against a wall, frightened of his own damn self. The handle of vodka in the cabinet over the stove was the only thing that calmed his nerves, there at the end.

—*the long walk isn't really that long at all*
—*it's ten feet from a holding cell to the execution room*

"What do you remember?" she asked.

"Him screaming himself to death."

"That's about right," she said. "I've been thinking over the last few days. You know, he really needed to go to the hospital, but he got to a point where he wouldn't have let me even if I'd known to take him. He'd gone through episodes before but never one that lasted that long. I kept hoping he'd snap out of it. He used to lay there and talk to your grandma like she was standing right next to his bed."

—*when it's time, the prisoner is called by their last name*
—*"it's time to go to the next room"*

"I remember the day he died," Dale said.

"Simmons had to go in to get him. I don't even think he was a sergeant, yet. He volunteered to go in there for me. I couldn't." She pursed her lips and closed her eyes. Then, suddenly, "Is there a coffee shop downstairs? I had to guzzle my latte because the nurse said I wasn't allowed to bring it in."

"Did you tell Charlie to send me here?"

"I told Charlie that neither of you were safe as long as you were spiraling the way you were, and that's the truth."

"Well," Dale said. "She did the right thing, then."

A man started yelling bloody murder down the hall, making both of them jump. The screams slowly formed into a horrible string of curses, making the nurses scramble to calm the patient down and, amazingly, he and his mother locked eyes and laughed like they were just sitting in a booth at Austin's Grill on his lunch break, eating burgers.

When Sarah came in and told them that visiting hours were over, his mother put a hand on his shoulder, and he put his hand on top of it. She told him that she loved him. She told him she was proud of him. She told him that Charlie loved him, and yes, that she would tell Charlie that he loved her, and that he wanted her to come see him as soon as she felt up to it.

He felt overwhelmingly lonely when she signed the clipboard, took her bag from the security guard, and walked out of the double doors. Dale wanted to follow her out of here, out of his own mind, back to a time when genetic probability meant nothing to him except a Punnett square on a biology exam that neither he nor Gentry would pass.

He thought about asking if Sarah could come and sit with him for a few minutes, just so he could feel a presence in the room, but decided to try to stick it out on his own.

Machines beeped in other rooms. Nurses shuffled back and forth, still trying to silence the strange shrieking voice down the hall. Wheelchairs crept on the tile, and the television in the hall played soap operas and game shows and commercials about mesothelioma and asbestos. Dale got up and used the bathroom again. The diarrhea had stopped. He was empty, and when it was time to eat, he pushed his dinner tray of food away.

He was still sitting there in the common area when he heard the voice, clear as day.

You can't blame her for not coming. You're an abuser.

"I am not," Dale said out loud. It was the first time the word had ever entered his mind.

What do you think yelling and carrying on and throwing things is?

He looked at Sarah as she brushed applesauce off of Mr. Louis's chin.

"Shut the fuck up," Dale said, a little too loudly. Sarah looked at him, sadly, with the look of a woman who has no idea how she can help a man she cares about. He had a feeling he'd seen that look before. He had a feeling he would remember that look for a long time.

There were three pills in his cup at bedtime: an anti-psychotic and two tablets of lithium.

 —three different drugs used for lethal injections, in this order:
 —sodium thiopental to cause unconsciousness
 —Pavulon to cause paralysis
 —potassium chloride to stop the heart

Charlie had peed on the stick. He just knew it. She had peed, and there were two lines, and he could feel her frowny face from here. Two lines for bipolar. That's how it worked. Dale would happily commit to another seventy-two hours if they'd just let him speak to her, to tell her goodnight, to ask her to come see him, to tell her whatever it was he was supposed to tell her to make this go away, starting with "let's never eat spaghetti again."

Dale reached for the nightstand, the place where a cell phone should have been. His fingers bumped a pile of broken crayons and they clattered to the floor. He pushed the printer paper with his notes off too, for good measure.

He was awakened an hour or two later by a woman's voice out in the common area.

"Where's my buddy?" The words were drawn out, like the person was talking to a baby. "Where's my best friend?"

Dale got out of bed, with only some difficulty, and cracked the door to look out. Mr. Louis was sitting straight up in his chair, skeleton arms flapping happily at a nurse creeping theatrically across the tile toward him. He smiled, grunting, moving back and forth in his seat, showing toothless gaps in his crooked teeth. "Where's my buddy?" she said, putting her hand against her forehead, pretending to look around. "Where is he?"

Mr. Louis grunted happily, waving his arms.

"Oh, there he is! Where have you been hiding?" she said.

"Good God," Dale said, amazed.

"My best buddy," the girl said. "Were you hiding?" She snuck behind Mr. Louis' armchair. He sat up with a straight back, mouth opened in sheer joy but saying nothing. She jumped out and said boo! He laughed. Then they both covered their faces and played a long, clumsy game of peek-a-boo.

Dale stepped out of his room to watch. A tennis-balled walker shuffled in place behind him. "Well I'll be damned," a man with wild hair said completely lucid, staring intently. "What's next?"

Shanice came in at five again to take his vitals. She asked him how he was feeling. His left hand was not shaking when he lifted it to let her pull the blood-pressure cuff onto his arm.

Dale tried to go back to sleep when she left, but found it difficult to contain his desire to start the day somehow. So he stayed sitting up in bed and spent a few minutes counting things: the ceiling tiles, the floor tiles, his heartbeats. There were thirty-one orange streetlights in the parking lot. Then he wandered out into the common area, even though no one else was awake, and found a worn-out crime novel fished out of a donation bin. He settled into a chair across from Mr. Louis. When he got to page fifty or so, the nurses leaned the old man's chair back until it was completely horizontal and changed his diaper. Dale used the book to waft away the smell of prunes and baby food and shit.

He couldn't remember the last time he had read fifty pages of anything in one sitting. Every time he reached the end of a chapter without getting distracted, he congratulated himself.

The nurses behind the desk were putting pills in little cups. Every now and then, someone would wake up alone in the dark and scream in terror down the hall, and they'd all go running. Judging by the fact that his mother's name was the only one on the visitor's log, he could deduce that most of these patients were here because their families were simply tired of dealing with them. This is what happened to people who didn't die of heroin overdoses or scream themselves to death in their forties. They ended up here. Mr. Louis was staring at the ceiling blankly. He never even blinked. Dale started looking up occasionally at his chest to make sure he was still breathing.

A year and a half ago, Charlie had walked down the aisle to him in a white cocktail dress she'd ordered off of Amazon, lace on the sleeves and skirt. Their fantasy involved increasingly comfortable houses, a dog, a cat, holidays at his mother's house, vacations in Beaufort, and a trip to Europe every three or four years. Now he'd give anything just to walk freely through a pharmacy, waiting for his little white prescription paper to be filled. He'd take whatever they prescribed him just to get his life back. He'd take a dozen pills, a hundred if he had to. God, in his mind, she was beautiful—dark hair, blue eyes, walking bent over with her elbows resting on a shopping cart filled with cereal and vitamins. Maybe she'd be touching noses with a baby in the seat while they waited for the tiny, magical orange bottles that would make him and keep him okay.

The other patients wandered out of their rooms. A nurse rolled Lucy up to a table. She was drooling and staring off into the distance like she was still asleep with her eyes open. Dale closed his book and walked over. "Can I sit here?" he asked.

Her face popped on like a light bulb. "Oh, absolutely, baby. I want to get to know you."

"My name is Dale."

"My name's Lucy," she said again. "I seen you around."

"I'm not mad anymore," he said.

"Ain't no reason to be mad. I ain't mad. You gonna die?"

"Probably not for a while."

"Ain't no reason to be mad, then."

Breakfast trays arrived on a rolling shelf. Dale stood up, found the tray with a sticker that said Lucy Nelson, and sat it down in front of her. "Well, thank you," she said.

He found his own tray on the rack and sat down. He didn't remember circling oatmeal and fried eggs on the menu yesterday, but he must have. He didn't mind. They'd given him fresh fruit as well. He pushed the grapes off to the side and ate the pineapple.

The mysterious shrieking voice rang deafeningly down the hall, the one Dale had been hearing since he arrived. The tortured, terrified sound gave Dale a shudder up his back. Another nurse was feeding Mr. Louis applesauce a few feet away, catching the applesauce on his chin and dragging it back up to his mouth where he gaped for it like a fish. Dale couldn't help but stare.

"Like feeding a baby," Dale said.

"I got two babies," Lucy said, her plastic spoon bending under the weight of her hand. "They grown."

The screams started to form phrases. Two nurses got up to investigate.

"People here got lots of problems," Lucy said. "Lots of problems, Lord Jesus, help us."

The man down the hall yelled, "No, I don't have to listen to you bitches!"

Lucy calmly struggled to tear open a sugar packet.

"Shit, shit, shit, shit," the man said in his room. "Is someone going to help us?"

"He crazy as a road lizard," Lucy whispered to Dale. The sugar exploded, covering everything on her tray, even the eggs. She flicked the packet to the floor.

The nurses walked around the corner guiding a disheveled, angry old man on a walker. White hair stuck out from his head, mad-scientist style, like he'd put a paper clip into a light socket.

"Shit, shit, shit, shit." He looked at Dale. "Are you going to help us?"

Dale stared.

"Someone help us! What exactly are we doing here? What's next?"

Sarah Hatcher slid a breakfast tray from the shelf. Dale hadn't seen her arrive. "Mr. Joe?" she said. "It's all right, honey.

How about you eat, and we'll read to you when you're done? "

"What are we doing next? Shitty shit, shit."

"Here's your food, Mr. Joe. Mmm, those are some good-looking pancakes."

"I bet you will, bitch. I bet you will. Are you going to help us?"

"Mr. Joe, can you sit down for me?"

"You're a shit, shit, shit, shit." They were more punctuated now, rhythmic, like an echo.

"Lord but that man tests my patience," Lucy said once Joe finally started accepting bites of food from Sarah.

During group, the same resident as before brought mandalas to color for relaxation. Dale smiled and thanked her when she put one in front of him. He shared a box of crayons with Lucy and didn't break any. Mr. Joe asked if the "bitch nurse" could come sit and color, so Sarah smiled weakly and walked over from the desk.

"You can sit here," Lucy said to Sarah, patting the table next to her.

"Thank you, Lucy. How are you feeling, Officer Overton?"

"Hungry as a horse," Dale admitted. Lucy had taken to snatching up every crayon he put down—despite the fact that she had at least twenty others at her disposal—so he started laying them right beside her so they'd be easier for her to grab.

"That's a good sign," Sarah said. "And Miss Lucy, how are you? Did you make friends with Mr. Dale?"

"Yeah, I bet you will, you bitch," Mr. Joe said, a few tables over. Sarah jumped.

"How about you watch what you say, mister?" Dale said. "There are ladies here."

Mr. Joe scratched nervously at his ear and turned back around.

"Sarah, how are your girls?" Dale asked. "I see Emma around town a lot." She was a cute little squirt, always grinning like she knew secrets that could ruin lives.

"Sarah, you got babies?" Lucy said, amazed.

"I got two babies," Sarah said.

"Two babies," Lucy said. "I got two babies!"

Dale said, "I never see your other one, though. Is it Abigail?" He legitimately didn't know if he'd be able to pick her out of a crowd if he had to.

"Abigail, yeah," Sarah said, not looking at him. "Real quiet, keeps to herself. She goes to school and comes straight home, stays inside a lot." Sarah picked up a new crayon and got the entire label off in one peel. "She's a Daddy's girl," she said, more to herself.

Dale didn't like the way she said it. He liked even less the way she avoided his eyes when she did. In that moment he remembered that he had taken an oath that included scanning the faces of the citizens in his town, to read their eyes their eyes and their mouths and their hands. Sarah had a swollen place on her lip, covered with the type of gooey lipstick that Charlie refused to wear because it made kissing him feel slimy.

When she went back to the nurse's desk, Dale said to Lucy, "I didn't like her husband before and I like him even less now."

Lucy pinched at the edges of her mandala with her clumsy fingers and finally lifted it up, examining it delicately. "Pretty," Lucy said.

"It's pretty," he confirmed.

At eleven, they dispersed back to their own rooms to meet with the doctors. Dale was sitting up in bed when they walked in, hands folded on his lap. "How are you feeling, Mr. Overton?" the female doctor asked him. Her name was Dr. Perry.

"I read a book this morning," he said, by way of an answer. "I honestly can't remember the last time I read a book."

"What book was it?" she asked, somewhat distracted by the clipboard in her hands.

"I don't remember the name," Dale said.

"Do you mind if we ask a few questions?"

"Go ahead."

"Do you feel like others are out to harm you? Do you feel paranoid about interpersonal relationships? Do you feel unnecessarily aggressive toward other people? Any homicidal thoughts or thoughts to harm yourself? Thoughts of death? Can you see or hear things that other people cannot see or hear?" Dale hesitates before answering this one, then slowly shook his head. "Do you find yourself speaking too quickly or repeating yourself? Any thoughts that life is not worth living?"

Dale could honestly answer no to every one of them.

"Well, it seems like you're feeling better," the male doctor said. He was incredibly fit and very young—no older than Dale but with three clusters of letters behind his name: Dr. Packer. Dale realized that everyone in his room was equal in the goal of protecting the people they liked *and* the people they didn't, the people who appreciated them *and* the people who didn't.

"I am," Dale said truthfully, trying very hard to look convincing while not looking like he was trying to look convincing. "Looking forward to going home, setting some things straight."

"I'm going to put in for your discharge tomorrow, if you're comfortable with that," Dr. Packer said.

"God, yes," Dale answered.

The two of them spent a minute fussing over a clipboard.

"Can you give me a name of someone we can call to come pick you up?" Dr. Packer asked.

He knew he should put down his mother's name, to be safe,

but his mother was not the person he wanted to see.

"Charlie Overton," he said, and recited her cell number.

"We'll give her a call," Dr. Packer said. "Discharges usually process by noon."

"Can I ask you two a question?"

Dr. Perry put the clipboard underneath her arm. "Sure."

"If you've got one parent that's bipolar, what's the chance that a kid will have it?" They stared at him awkwardly. "Like . . . my dad had something, but my mom didn't, and I do. So, if I have it and my wife doesn't, what are the odds that the kid will? Is it fifty-fifty, or what?"

Dr. Packer shook his head. "Oh, no. I mean, we do think it's genetic to an extent, because it does seem to run in families, but it's hard to put a specific percentage to it. The disorder depends on other factors."

"Is there a test for it?" Dale said. "Like can you test the kid when it's born and start treating it early?"

"It doesn't usually manifest until the early twenties," Dr. Packer said. "And it's not really the kind of thing we can check for in a blood test."

"Okay. Thanks anyway," Dale nodded, feeling no better.

They made an appointment for him at a psychiatry office in the city in a week. He promised to go. They asked him which pharmacy he wanted his medicines sent to. He promised to take them. They gave him brochures for "loved ones" of mental health patients and he promised he'd pass them along. He asked where he could get a few more, to give to families, in case he bumped into any of these problems in his work. He wondered how many domestic dispute calls had mental illness at the center of them.

Then Dale shook both of their hands and told them thank you.

Living with it would be like standing in the center of a see-saw with one foot on each side, trying to keep it level. Dale hated his father growing up, for things he didn't understand, things he only barely understood now. Dale didn't know the word manic when he was nine, watching grape jelly pooling in the cracks of white linoleum. He didn't know the word depressive when his father was too exhausted to shower, go to work, or eat. He didn't know the word psychotic when his father laid in bed yelling and throwing things and carrying on and dying, his skin boiling, his lungs gasping, his blood toxic until the last moment, his final words something along the lines of, "Get away, get away."

Not *go* away. *Get* away.

Dale did not want to tell anyone in his life that they needed to get away from him. Dale wanted to go home and flip the calendar in their kitchen to the right date. He wanted to hold his wife, and have sex with her on days when he didn't have to. He wanted to keep a closer watch on Sarah's family and he wanted to spend more time with his mother. Dale felt exiled from his life, imprisoned for someone else's crimes, and he didn't have a plan for how to sneak back in. He could only hope that Charlie would let him.

Of course she would.

He went back out into the common area and wrote a clumsy love note to her, in crayon, on a clean piece of hospital printer paper.

Lucy was still at the table, coloring a new mandala.

"They're discharging me tomorrow," he said.

She looked sad. "And I was just getting to know you."

"I've got to get home now. I've got a wife. She may even be pregnant."

She looked up, happily. "A baby?"

"Maybe."

"Boy, how you gonna not know if you have a baby or not?" she said. Dale smiled and rolled a crayon back and forth between his hands. Mr. Joe watched them irritably at the next table and Mr. Louis's bottom lip hung down, hands bent against his chest like he was practicing for his coffin. "My Jada grown, got three babies. Hunter I ain't seen in five years. Don't know if he will come see me."

"What are you doing, fat ass?" Joe asked, staring at Lucy.

"Watch your mouth," Dale said, in his best cop voice. "That's your last warning, sir."

Lucy perked up, "You think you can come see me in a few weeks when we out of here?"

"Sure, Lucy," Dale said. "My wife and I will come to see you."

"McLean's Funeral Home," she said. "That's where I'll be. It's the cheapest. Pretty green carpet, though, like a Christmas tree."

"Who the fuck do you think you are?" Joe said, before Dale could answer.

Dale stood up so fast his chair flew back with a loud squeal. He towered over the old man, glaring hard enough to make him shrink back.

Sarah came over. "Mr. Joe, let's go ahead and get you a nap, how about that?"

The old man looked at Dale, who was holding fast to his "don't fuck with me" face. Joe stood up and took the handles of his walker, shuffling down the hall. Sarah followed a few steps back, and Dale after her in case Joe wanted to get belligerent.

When he was in bed, Sarah gave Dale a squeeze on the shoulder. "Thanks, honey."

"It's nothing. Let me know if you need anything," he said.

"I appreciate it," she said with that sad, fake cheerfulness that represented her entire state of being.

"And Sarah," he said, trying to find the right words. He would need them later. "I know I haven't been myself. I'm sorry for a lot of things I've done and said. I would make excuses, and I probably have one or two good ones, but you knowing that I'm legitimately sorry is more important." Sarah looked down at the floor, wrung her hands in front of her for a moment. Then, she did something he never expected. She made legitimate eye contact with him, something she hadn't done since he was a boy. Her gaze was soft but scrutinizing and a little bit cold. "But mainly I'm sorry if there's anything outside of here that's gone . . . unnoticed. I'll try to keep a better eye on things."

She was silent.

"I mean it." Dale looked her in the eye. "If you or your kids need anything, you call me. Whether I'm on duty or not, you call me. You understand?"

"You've got more important things going on," she said, quietly.

"No," he said firmly. "No, I don't."

Dale was too excited to sleep. He turned the small lamp back on and reached over to the nightstand to tear a corner off of a half-finished piece of printer paper about gas chambers. He wrote his phone number on it for Lucy and, after fifteen minutes trying to figure out what to say to her, determined "See you in a few weeks" was best.

He decided to get up early tomorrow so he could take his time getting ready to see Charlie again, getting ready to show her the new him, or (more importantly) the *old* him. Dale would shower, and they would bring him the clothes they'd taken from him when he was admitted, and he would put on his own jeans, his own t-shirt, socks, and sneakers. He wanted Charlie to see him as a real man, wearing real clothes, hearing only real voices. Dale would say goodbye to Mr. Louis, who would not acknowledge his presence, and even Mr. Joe, who would probably call him a Shitty Shit Shit. He would apologize to Shanice the same way he'd apologized to Sarah, because he didn't want to walk out and never see her again and carry that guilt with him for the rest of his life. He would tell Charlie tomorrow, when she came to pick him up, that he'd never bring anything like that into their home again.

Dale turned the light out and put himself to sleep imagining the beep of the swipe machine behind the desk that would open the double doors, a rush of sterilized hospital wind from the hallway combing his short hair back. The elevator down the hallway will open, and the sleepy snake in his stomach will lift and drop harmlessly just before he arrives on the ground floor. He will emerge victorious, chin lifted, a love note for Charlie in his fist. The occupants of the hospital lobby will give him knowing smiles and the occasional "go get 'em, tiger" nod as he walks past them to meet his wife.

And with amazing speed and accuracy, on his way out of the door, he will run through a list in his head of everywhere he and his wife could possibly stop and eat on the way home, a kind of post-crucifixion communion, something to celebrate his botched execution—burgers, or Mexican, don't you like Mexican, well I had Mexican the other day but it wasn't good Mexican, and don't you want good Mexican, or there's that little Italian place you like so much, and I could go for some Italian, but it's your day sweetheart, it's your day, we can go wherever you want, how about a grilled cheese and tomato soup from Austin's, maybe that would be good for your stomach if you're eating for two, right? Did you think I wouldn't figure it out? I'm happy. Oh God, sweetheart, I'm so happy.

And Dale will walk to freedom, out of the front doors of the hospital, back into the sunshine. He will do everything a man can do to make it so this never happened. He will leave the hospital ready to make sure this whole experience is nothing but a small bump in the story of his marriage and his life.

What he will not expect to see, when he squints into the sun toward the parking lot, is the sight of his mother walking down the sidewalk toward him instead of his wife. Her eyes are sad and apologetic. She is shaking her head.

OUT OF OUR SUFFERING

YESTERDAY MS. ATKINS HANDED OUT "the Cask of Amontillado" during literature time. She told us that the principal at her last school said the story was too hard for third graders but that no child should go to middle school not knowing what bullying means or how to handle it right. By the end of the story I was not sure who was the bully or what the right way to handle bullying was but I knew I wanted to tie my daddy's hunting dog to a tree until she starved to death. Cole Tanner couldn't say Amontillado and kept saying armadillo and Ms. Atkins made him put his name on the board.

When I got home I ate supper like everything was normal and watched the show about people who live in city apartments then I went to the shed. I tied a rope right around Loretta's neck since I've seen her slip out of her collar before. The two of us went way into the woods past the deer stand on the other side of Coolie's pond and I cow-knotted her to a good tree and walked away. She stood there watching me leaving her with a stupid look in her eyes.

This morning my eyes are glued shut with gunk. I am

cleaning all the crumbled worksheets out of the bottom of my book bag on the porch when Daddy comes out of the shed and says "Where's Loretta?"

"I don't know. I went looking for her last night," I say.

"Probably chased a possum into the woods," he says and lights a cigarette. He tells us all the time that he will never love anything as much as he loves that dog and I wonder if loving a dog that much makes you a good person. She was one thousand and eleven dollars plus a hundred more for all her shots.

I go to Bethany Elementary School just like every other kid in town. My stomach hurts on the bus but it's a different kind of pain than the kind that makes you throw up. It's like someone is poking around inside me with a knife. Ms. Atkins makes us pronounce the Latin part of the "Cask of Amontillado" over and over: *nemo me impune lacessit.* Nee-moh may imp-you-nay lah-kess-it. It means that if someone hurts you, you should always hurt them back.

Mama is frying up liver pudding and eggs when I get home from school. We have breakfast for supper about three times a week but we don't get breakfast for breakfast except on Christmas so I don't mind. I hear the toaster pop so I know there won't be pancakes. Her foot catches on the plastic part of the floor that is bent up from the damp beneath our doublewide and she slams her head into a cabinet and says goddamn it.

She wouldn't have said it if Daddy was in the house or he'd tell the preacher on Sunday. Then we'd all have to stand on the porch of the church and listen to Pastor Ryan talk about what happens to people who don't give God the respect He deserves. One time he talked until even the choir ladies left and they usually hang around gabbing until the basketball game has already started.

Abigail is seven years older than me. She is the queen of the house, or that's what she wants you to believe. She sits at the desk in her and Daddy's room and does homework until Mama goes in and tells her to come be social. Abigail never asks to have friends over so school is the only time she talks to anyone except for when she's going at me. One day she told me I was an accident and when I asked her what that meant she said nevermind. I asked Mrs. Weston what it means to be an accident and her eyes got all sad and she said that it means that I am a miracle.

Loretta is an outside dog so no one will worry too much about her tonight but I don't know how long it takes dogs to starve. I feel like if I went without food I'd die in a few hours but I like to eat. I am trying to get a body like Abigail's because she looks like a model in Daddy's white tank tops, all hips and tits since she got her period and he said that she was a woman now. That's why she gets to slept in the big bed with him and I sleep on the couch. Hopefully Loretta will starve before long because all hell will bust loose if he figures out what I did. I go to my red chair in the living room and root around in my book bag for the Amontillado story to read before supper. We have to underline the words we don't know like afflicted and grotesque and crypt and look them up in a dictionary.

Mama comes in and starts fanning herself with her apron. She has been at the hospital where she works since four o'clock in the morning and she looks dog tired. Daddy comes in wiping his hands on a rag. I ask him what insufferable means and point to the word on the paper. He goes behind my chair and reads what it says. "It's what hell is," he says. "Something so terrible that you can't stand it for another minute. Like your Mama."

She looks at him but doesn't say anything. He gets that

nastiness in his eyes and stares her down. Then he pokes his lip out like she's hurt his feelings. "See? She doesn't even talk to me. Acts like she's too good to talk to your sweet old pops," he says.

"She's a big fat bitch," I say.

Mama and Daddy hate each other but not the kind of hate you see on TV when the wife and husband fight over who is cooking supper and who is sleeping on which side of the bed and then they kiss and the audience laughs. It is not like that at all. One time my daddy used a vacuum cleaner like a baseball bat to beat the tar out of Mama and when she fell down all the dirt landed on her and she looked like a dead person partway buried. One time he threw his mug of hot coffee in her face and took Abigail into the bedroom and the two of them didn't come out for two days.

When they fight it is like those cartoons where the ground is glue. I cannot move even to blink so I have to stand there and watch whatever happens. Abigail's legs work fine so she runs but always comes back for me if she can. When I told my aunt in a letter that it makes me scared when they fight she wrote back and said "Your daddy is a good man and this is his way of trying to make things work. Your mama will realize that eventually."

It happens more often now that Daddy doesn't have a real job and when he gets angry it feels like the whole house is on fire and the ground is going to swallow us right up because God will decide that we are too nasty to live on earth and Hell is a better place for us. Loretta is probably laid down in a bed of leaves right now wondering when I am coming back to get her. Even though I did the right thing by tying her out there it feels like I'm the one who's dying instead.

Today everyone had ants in their pants after recess and Ms. Atkins yelled at Cole Tanner to sit down and shut up. When people yell I get sweaty and sometimes I pee my pants a little even if they're not mad at me. My body can get scared of a thing even when my brain isn't scared of it at all and that is what I hate most about myself. My heart feels like a bird slamming into a window trying to get out even though I am cool as a cucumber. I raise my hand and say "May I go see Mrs. Weston?" like I am supposed to and Ms. Atkins tells me to take the hall pass and go.

Mrs. Weston is my guidance counselor. She's got big hair like Dolly Parton and no lips. Her husband is Austin who owns the grill in town and if I go there and tell him I didn't get any lunch he'll give me a grilled cheese that is dripping with butter and that is my favorite. I think he probably knows I always get lunch but he gives me one anyway with this sad look on his face that a lot of people give me before they're about to do something special for me. I like when people are sad for me and I like being in the hallway during class when I am the only one there and everyone else is trapped in their rooms doing flashcards or popcorn reading or multiplications. I feel like I am at a zoo watching the animals but I can do what I please. Wolves are my favorite animals because they can live in families but they can survive on their own if they are strong enough.

The guidance office is yellow with chairs and a couch. There are paintings on the wall of flowers and fields with flowers in them and flowers in vases and people holding flowers and there are fresh flowers on the desk and on all the tables in the waiting area and it all reminds me of the funeral of the boy who died from his needles years ago. There's a fish tank bubbling in the corner making a nice sound that would put me to sleep if I had time to lay down.

Mrs. Weston pokes her Dolly Parton head out of her office and by now I am not sweating and my heart is quiet but I don't want to tell her because she will make me go back to class. I have been seeing her since Abigail backhanded me at home and I got the bruise on my face and Ms. Atkins told the office that I was at risk.

Mrs. Weston holds up a laminated poster with a bunch of faces on it. She asks me how I'm feeling today and I point to the one with the angry eyes. She asks me what I'm angry about and I say that Ms. Atkins yelled at Cole Tanner.

"Do you think Cole Tanner deserved to be yelled at?"

"He's a shit," I say.

"Where did you learn to call people shits?"

"Everyone calls people shits."

She leans forward in her seat like I am a good movie. "Do your Mama and Daddy call each other shits?" I say no. "Do they call you a shit?" I say no. "What was it about Cole Tanner getting yelled at that made you angry?"

"I got sweaty and my heart got going and my stomach hurts."

"Can you point to where it hurts?"

I touch my belly button. This is what I do whenever any doctor asks me where my stomach hurts like I'm going to point to my knee or something. It is not a pain that comes and stays but when it comes it hurts bad enough to make my whole body go hard for a few seconds but I don't know how to tell her this. She says uh-huh and writes something down.

"I am angry because my mama is mean to my daddy," my mouth says all of a sudden.

She looks at me over the edge of her glasses. "How is your mama mean to your daddy?"

"She looked really good before she got married. Skinny and

pretty hair. But she let herself go after she had the kids and now she's a lazy fat ass and I can't stand to look at her much less touch her or have her in my bed after she's worked with them goddamn loonies at the hospital."

Mrs. Weston says in a sad voice, "Emma, is that really how you feel about your mama?"

"She is *insufferable*."

Mrs. Weston looks like I punched her straight in her mouth and I'm not sure if that is a good thing for me or not. She says that's enough for one day, but she will talk to Ms. Atkins to make sure it's okay if I come back next week.

When I'm in the hallway by myself I like to only step on the red tiles, or take the whites two at a time, or pretend the black ones are lava. I look in the windows at the other students and when they see me out by myself I give them a "haha" smile because I am clever enough to get out of class whenever I want and they are not. It is not so bad to be at risk.

When I get home Daddy is under Sammy Cotter's pickup. Since the garage closed downtown he fixes trucks and cars in our garage to make money. He says everyone else in the house is lazy and living on his hard work and he breaks his back to put food on our table and clothes on our asses and what thanks does he get? Mama told him a few weeks ago that her job at the hospital pays more bills than his did even when he had a job and let's just say no one talks about who has a job and who doesn't anymore.

Daddy shimmies out from under the belly of the truck where he's laying on a folded up towel and says "You seen Loretta today?" and I say "No sir" and he grunts a little and rolls away.

I need to wash my dirty panties. Mama's car isn't in the

driveway and Abigail is reading at her desk eating a pack of fruit snacks so I know no one will see me. The pain in my stomach is bad but I don't know who I should tell. I decide to just let it work itself out. That is what my Mama says when there is a problem. "It'll work itself out."

Most people don't know what couches look like on the inside but I do because I sleep on the couch. If you lift up the cushions there are pockets and zippers where you can keep things and no one will ever find them. If Abigail makes Daddy mad he says he's going to put me in the bed with him and make her sleep on the couch and then she stops whatever she is doing to make him mad.

I don't mind not having a room for myself because the whole trailer is my room. Mama does my laundry and folds it and keeps it in stacks on the kitchen floor against the wall so I don't need a dresser or closet and everything else I have fits in the couch. I keep my McDonald's toys, my Barbie, my deck of cards, and my beaded jump rope under the right cushion and my *World Book* "C" encyclopedia and letters from my Gamma under the left one. I keep my messed up panties in grocery bags way in the back past the cushions until I can sneak them into the washing machine. I don't want anyone in the house to know I am in the third grade and I still pee my pants when I get scared, especially not Abigail who will make fun of me to no end or Daddy who will get mad at Mama for not teaching me any better even though she taught me good enough but I just can't help it sometimes.

There are four dirty panties in there since I last washed them. They smell to high heaven when I dump them into the washing machine and turn it on.

"You doing laundry?" Abigail says from Daddy's room.

"Do you hear the washing machine?" I say.

"Shut up you little shit."

I go to check on Loretta and she wags her tail and stands up. She is panting a lot but she's bouncing around tugging on the rope to get to me. I stay a few feet away from where she'd be able to jump on me. "Do you know my daddy loves you more than he loves anything?" She swings her tail back and forth and goes down on her front legs like she wants to play and barks twice. She doesn't look hungry to me yet. Something wet happens between my legs even though I didn't feel myself pee at all.

When I walk back home I move my panties from the washer into the dryer. Mama is in her bedroom changing out of her work clothes but she hasn't checked the laundry yet. She's got stuff on the counter to make spaghetti with meat sauce and I hope there's butter toast and stinky cheese to go with it.

I go to the bathroom and pull my pants down and there is a chunk of blood in my panties about as long as my thumb. A few months ago Ms. Atkins took us to a health center and they separated the girls and boys and talked to us about boobs and vaginas so I know I am a woman now. The first person I want to tell is Abigail but I know she will say something that will make me mad. I root around in the kitchen cabinet for a grocery bag so I can put the bloody panties under the couch cushion until I can figure out what to do with them. Someone slams the trashcan lid shut behind me and scares me to death. When I turn around Abigail sees me holding a wad in my hand and comes toward me and I don't bother backing away. She peels open my fingers and sees the panties with blood on them and something comes over her. She hits me so hard that it feels like my head turns all the way around like an owl. My eyes start watering even though I am not sad but angry.

Abigail grabs the panties and wraps them in a grocery bag

while I am still trying to stand then throws the bag into the trashcan. "Were you going to hide them in the couch like your piss-pants?" Her voice is nasty.

"Shut up," I say, scared.

Abigail jerks me up by my arm and takes me into the bathroom and closes the door. She pushes me toward the toilet and roots around in the cabinet and pulls a white stick out of a box. I know it's a tampon and I know what tampons are for but I wasn't listening very hard the day Ms. Atkins explained how to use it because I thought maybe I would be special and not have to.

Abigail unwraps it and gives it to me. I stare at the little teeth at the end. "It won't hurt," she says. "You put the thick part in you and then push the thin part and it makes the thing come out."

It makes sense but it doesn't make me feel any better about sticking something like that up inside me. Abigail turns around and I take down my pants and sit on the commode. I put the thing between my legs and wiggle it around but nothing happens. I push the thin part with my thumb and the whole thing falls into the toilet.

"Dumbass," Abigail says and fishes another one out of the box. "Try again. Don't push it until it's in."

"How do I know when it's in?"

"You'll know."

So I unwrap the new tampon and move it in circles until it finally finds the right place to slide in. I push the thin stick with my thumb and it goes inside of me. Then I pull the plastic part out and Abigail turns around and takes it from me like she is not even holding something gross. She puts it back into the wrapper.

"See how I did that?" she says. "Then you wrap it in toilet paper, the same way you wrap your panties so no one can see what's inside."

"Okay," I say. When I bend down to pull my jeans back up, I can feel it thick and hard inside of me. It hurts.

"You gotta change it every six hours."

"Okay," I say.

"Don't tell anyone," she said, looking me in the eye. "Not Daddy or Mama."

"Okay."

"If you get your panties bloody throw them away."

"Okay."

"Give me a day or two to figure things out."

I don't know what she means but I say okay. She leaves me standing there sore between my legs with my cheek busted open from the dime store ring on her hand.

We eat our spaghetti later in the living room. Mama sits on the floor and Abigail sits on the couch with Daddy and I sit in my armchair. Daddy finishes what's on his plate and sops up the sauce with his buttered toast then goes into the kitchen for seconds. Mama doesn't eat much and Abigail is picking at her food like a bird. Daddy and I are the fastest eaters in the house and we eat the most by far. Sometimes Mama jokes and says, "No one's going to take it from you."

"Y'all seen Loretta today?" Daddy asks from the kitchen.

"No sir," Abigail says. I stay quiet.

"We could call Dale," Mama says. "He'd help us look."

"Officer Overton?" Abigail asks. "He came to our school last week to do the drug talk." Abigail stops eating and stares off like something very far away just became more interesting than what's sitting in front of her. I've met Officer Overton a bunch of times around town, except when he went on his real long vacation to Mama's hospital, and I remember Mama helping out with his wedding. I got to help clean up afterward and when we were done his new wife whose name I cannot remember let me keep a bunch of the fake flowers but after a while I threw them away.

"I think someone stole her," Daddy says. "Good dog, purebred. Loretta was one thousand and eleven dollars."

"Plus a hundred more for all her shots," Abigail says like the words to a song she's heard too many times.

"If someone stole her I swear to God there'll be hell to pay."

"What if someone stole me or Abigail?" I am trying to get his mind off of Loretta so he doesn't get any ideas about going and looking for her.

"I'd kill anyone who tried to take my babies away from me. I'd kill them for even thinking about it. I don't care who it is."

Mama puts her fork down like she is full. I start thinking about all the ways my daddy could kill someone. I think about poor Fortunato being walled up with bricks in a hole.

"Is being buried alive a bad way to die?" I ask.

"I can't think of a worse way," Daddy says.

"What about getting shot?" I ask.

Mama sucks her teeth. "Emma Lynn, don't talk about people getting shot."

Daddy lets me shoot his Beretta in the woods and he says Mama can't say anything about it. He taught me how to stand with my legs in a stance and how to cup my left hand under my right even if that is not how they do it in the movies.

"Getting shot is better," Daddy says. "At least you don't suffer."

I slurp my spaghetti and Abigail stares at me all mean and tells me to straighten up. She's always acting high and mighty like she doesn't have to care about anything or anyone in the house as long as Daddy treats her like a princess. Plus I can still feel the tampon in me and the cut on my face and they make me angry at her too.

"What about starving to death?" I say.

"You'd go thirsty first," Daddy says. He's still not looking up from his food. "But that's a sorry way to die too. Worse than being buried alive."

"So starving or going thirsty is the worst way to die," I say.

"Making something suffer is worse than putting something out of its misery," he says. "That's why hunters need to shoot straight or the deer suffers and you've got to walk up to it and pop it in its head."

"Pop it in its head," I say.

After dinner Abigail sits at the desk squinting at a piece of paper because Daddy won't let a computer in the house. She writes as fast as she can like she is a person in a movie trying to move a satellite or turn off a bomb, like the whole world depends on how fast she can write.

I go with a flashlight to see Loretta after everyone goes to bed. She barks when she sees me and she has pulled on her rope so hard that it is making her neck bleed. Her brown fur is matted with red and her eyes are watering like she's been crying even though I know that dogs don't cry. She's panting and yelping and whining. I think about the tampon inside of me drinking up blood and I think about what Officer Overton is doing right now in his brick house with his wife whose name I still can't remember and maybe a kid too, like me, and I think about the ground opening up and somehow I know it's too late. I walk backward with my eye on Loretta until the flashlight beam can't find her anymore.

Abigail gives me four tampons before I get on the bus in the morning and tells me not to forget to change them. "Just get through today," she says, but I am not sure what will happen if I do or don't. When I can't hold my pee anymore I put a tampon in my sock and ask Ms. Atkins if I can go to the bathroom. I sit on the toilet and do the whole thing myself. I never knew why there were little trashcans in the stall but now I see that it's a good idea.

I get off of the bus on the way home and stop by Austin's and he throws a grilled cheese into the iron for me. My stomach feels emptied out but not like I'm hungry. The emptiness feels better than being full of food but I don't know why.

When I get into my pajamas after dinner, my shoulders are as soft as Abigail's. I even have an easier time brushing my hair because it is shining at the top. Ms. Atkins said that periods can make some girls look ugly but some girls have a period and look even prettier than they did before. That must be what happened to Abigail and maybe even me. I stare at myself in the mirror and like what I see which is not something I'm used to. I bet I will look like a model in a few months if I keep having periods like this one. I stay in the bathroom for maybe an hour painting my fingernails red and my toenails purple. I even get Abigail's green mud stuff and slather it all over my face. I wait for it to get hard and then I wash it off. I can't tell if it has changed my face at all but it felt good to do it anyway and that's enough.

The lights are all out when I come out of the bathroom feeling as pretty as I have ever felt. I go toward the couch to get some beauty sleep but I hear Abigail and Daddy talking in their bedroom. It's hard for anyone but me to sneak around because I am still light enough not to make the floor creak and I know where to step and where not to. I crouch to hear and Abigail makes a noise like a whining dog. I've heard it before and tonight it is louder than normal and it sounds like she is crying like a fussy baby. The noise makes my face turn hot and my hands sweat and I feel like our whole house does not belong to the world anymore but to some other place where nothing good will ever happen to us again. It gets in me and swims around in my empty stomach and between my legs like a poison.

After a few minutes I hear my Daddy grunt a few times and then he hollers out. He says fuck then neither of them say anything for a long time until he whispers something but I can't hear what it is. She says something back in a girly voice. He laughs and then they are quiet.

I don't turn the TV on when I lay down because I have a TV in my head tonight. I am a secret agent or a Power Ranger or a ninja assassin and I am not afraid of anything. If the ground opens to swallow us up I will flip out of the way and let my mama and daddy and Abigail get sucked down to Hell and then I'll figure out how to get right with God again for my own damn self.

When the clock says 1:37am Abigail comes out of their room and I pretend to be asleep. She comes right up to the couch. "Get a bag and put some clothes in it. Be quiet."

"Why?"

"I said so."

"Why?"

She snatches me up to show she is serious. Her nails dig into my wrist but I don't squeal. Abigail drags me into the kitchen and pushes me toward my stacks of clothes, then grabs one of the cloth grocery bags that you take to the store yourself to save the earth.

"Fill it," she says. "Pants, shirts, panties. I got your tooth-brush and some tampons." She goes to the closet and gets my coat while I do what she says. Then Abigail puts one hand on me and the other on the doorknob and she breathes out hard and opens the door. My whole body must be sweating because when the cold air hits the wet patches of my skin I start shaking. She closes the door as quietly as she can and gives me my coat. I put it on.

"Where are we going?"

"Be quiet," she says.

We walk a little ways down the driveway.

"What if I want to stay here?"

"Aunt Laura can give us enough money to go somewhere."

"Where is somewhere?" I ask.

"Emma shut up. Please."

I don't know if she has ever said please to me in my life. I stop moving and drop my grocery bag on the ground. "You're doing this because you think now that I have a period Daddy will want me in the bed and you will have to sleep on the couch," I say.

She grabs my arm and jerks me again. "Are you stupid?"

Before I can answer the back door of the trailer opens and Mama is standing there looking like she would not know which of Mrs. Weston's smiley faces to point to.

"No," she says like she is begging. "Not tonight."

Abigail pushes me behind her and says to Mama, "You stay, then. We're going."

"I'm not going," I say.

"Shut the fuck up," Abigail says.

I try to walk toward Mama but Abigail grabs the hood of

my coat and pulls me backward onto the ground and the wind goes out of me in a rush. Mama runs down the stairs like she wants to help me but Abigail gets in her way.

They look at one another for a long time then Abigail starts to cry and Mama starts to cry and I am on the ground still shaking bad from the cold. Mama snatches Abigail to her chest like she has never hugged anyone in her life and when I stand up Abigail grabs me against them with one arm. They are crying like someone has died. Then the porch light comes on and all of us jerk closer to one another.

When the back door opens Daddy is standing there in his boxers with his Beretta in his hand and we are standing in the orange circle that the porch light makes on the ground. Once he sees we are not criminals he looks closer and sees something much worse.

He doesn't say anything or move. He just stands in the doorway staring at Mama with the gun against his leg. She and Abigail are looking at him like he is the Devil come to earth and I can't help it but let go and pee runs down my leg.

"You girls go inside," he says, sweet as you please. "It's too cold to be out here."

We don't move.

Mama squeezes us. "Go inside." Her voice is peaceful.

Abigail starts walking but my feet are stuck like glue. I cannot stop staring at where Daddy is standing up above us on the porch with the big orange light behind him like a giant shadow. He exhales like he is getting impatient so Abigail turns around and picks me up under my armpits and I wrap my arms and legs around her even though I am too big to be toted.

She takes me right into the bathroom and puts me in the tub and closes the door. I still can't move or talk and my body is shaking like I am poor Fortunato trapped in the wall and oh God, Loretta, where's my mama? Abigail turns on the water in the sink and in the tub hard as it will go. She kneels down in front of me and covers my ears with her hands and when we are this close together I see we have the same color eyes.

I am supposed to ask my Sunday school class for prayers because my Mama is in the hospital from a terrible car crash and might not live. Daddy stands up during the service and asks the congregation to bow their heads and pray for her too. Abigail didn't say a word to him or me all last night so he put her on the couch and I got to sleep in the bed. He put one hand under my shirt and touched my chest and stomach hard. His body shook for a long time and when he hollered it sounded like he was mad at everything in the world.

Abigail doesn't bow her head when we pray for our Mama to overcome her injuries. She is staring off when Pastor Ryan says that trials happen because of the sin in our hearts and Daddy whispers "Yes Lord."

The pastor says that any person or family that wishes to renounce their sin and give themselves to God may come up to the altar and do so during the final hymn but no one ever does. The organist starts playing but Abigail does not sing this hymn and I never sing the hymns ever so Daddy is the only one singing "His Eye is on the Sparrow." He closes his eyes like the Spirit is in him and Mama always said that it didn't matter how loud or bad a person sings as long as they are singing with the Spirit and that's what my daddy does.

We get to the second verse and I look up and Abigail is crying so hard that her whole body is shaking. Daddy reaches over like a dad is supposed to do and she runs down the aisle as soon as he touches her shoulder. Abigail falls down a few feet in front of the altar in front of everyone with a thunk that I feel through my shoes. Pastor Ryan puts down his hymnal and puts his hand on her head like he wants to pray for her but she slaps his arm, then sits up on her knees and looks at the cross and I can tell that she is not giving herself to God or anyone else. Daddy stares at her confused and angry that she is making a spectacle of herself and that Mama isn't here to handle it for him.

After a minute Abigail looks over her shoulder at me. Since I have been at risk plenty of people have looked at me like they are sad before but no one has ever looked at me this way. Her eyes are in love and scared. We do not belong to God anymore and we can never belong to God again if we ever did to begin with. I walk down the aisle and the closer I get the harder she cries. She grabs me down onto her lap and rocks me back and forth while she cries and before I know it I am crying too just because seeing her cry is insufferable.

Pastor Ryan reaches out again to pray for us but Abigail gives him a look so ugly that he jerks his hand back like she burned him. She puts her face into my hair and keeps rocking me like she is trying to get me to go to sleep forever. She stares at the cross like if she could beg hard enough with her eyes God might reach down and pick us both up and carry us in his giant hand out of the church and into Heaven itself. But the song ends and the only giant hands we feel are the ones wrapping around our waists to pull us both up from the ground. My daddy says amen.

That night Daddy rolls me belly-up onto his chest and touches me while I stare at the ceiling fan going around. He is so busy with his hands on my stomach and legs that he doesn't hear Abigail leave. I hear her leave because she steps on all the wrong floorboards.

"It's better when you make noise," he says but I lay like a dead person on top of him until I am sure my sister is good and long gone. He digs between my legs with his fingers and growls like a bear and I hate him so much that my body wants to go off like a bomb and kill him. When he finally rolls me off of him I lay awake for a long time.

He doesn't even realize she's not there when he wakes up and goes out to the shed. It does not occur to him that she has left him forever and that it's just me and him now. He will not take me to the hospital to see my mama even though I have asked him three times and each time he has said, "Why? We don't need her fat ass around here, do we?"

"No, we don't need her fat ass around here."

I am sitting in my armchair with the "Cask of Amontillado" on my lap trying to do my homework before the bus comes to pick me up but I think about Loretta and throw up my cereal. My whole body is shaking like there is something to be afraid of but I'm not sure what that is anymore. Maybe I will just be scared of every little thing for the rest of my life, like I am made from fear and I'll never remember what it feels like to not be scared.

I'm thinking about a life like that when the gravel in the driveway crunches. I look out of the kitchen window and it is a police car. There is a piece of cereal stuck up in my nose from when I threw up.

Officer Overton is playing on the laptop in his car. When he sees me coming down the porch stairs he steps out and closes the door. He is big and handsome and looks like any good cop on TV. His hair is neat and his shoes are shiny and there is not a single wrinkle in his entire uniform that I can see even though I am sure he is the kind of man who beats up lots of bad guys and walks away from explosions without even turning around to look at them. Dale's wife must be a good wife to keep him looking so good.

"Emma?"

"Yes sir."

He walks with all the gizmos on his big belt squeaking and jangling. He says, "I was really sorry to hear about your mama."

I say, "We are praying that she gets better."

"From her car accident?" he says. He is looking at me the way my counselor does.

"Yes sir."

"I got a letter that I think is from your sister. Is she okay?"

"She's much better now," I say. The cereal in my nose finally falls back into my throat and I snort and swallow it. He pulls Abigail's letter out of his pocket and plays with it but I can't see what it says. His gun has a big, thick grip on it. "Is that a Glock?" I ask him.

He looks down at his waist. "Oh. Yeah."

"I like it."

"Thank you."

"I'm good with a Beretta."

"That's what I hear," Officer Overton says. "Where's your daddy?"

"In the shed."

He nods and looks over there to make sure I am telling the truth but then he looks back at me. Officer Overton points to my cheek where Abigail hit me with her ring a few days ago and looks at me hard. "Did you get hit?"

"No sir." But I did, and I wish Abigail was here to hit me again. My eyes start to burn and leak.

He goes all soft. "Hey, hey. That's all right. Can I ask what happened?"

"I got my period." I am scared of him and I don't know what to say. "I'm sorry. I got my period. I'm sorry."

"Happens to the best of us," he says with a quiet little laugh "That's okay."

"No it's not."

"Where's Abigail, Emma?"

"She's much better now," I say again. "I'm sorry."

Officer Overton kneels down so I am taller than him. "What are you sorry for?"

"Loretta," I say. My insides are going to go up my throat or out my ass one or the other.

"Who's Loretta?" he asks.

"I'm just sorry Abigail wrote you a letter and you had to come down here to where we live and deal with us."

"Can you look at me, Emma?"

I can't.

"Emma, can you look at me?"

I can't.

"I'm here because your sister asked for help. If something bad happens you should never be afraid to ask people like me for help. That's why we're here." His voice sounds like he is up high and I am falling way down into a hole. "That's why I'm here, right now. So I need for you to not be sorry that I'm here and to never be sorry if I come to see you. It's not your fault that I'm here and I'm here because I want to be."

"Yes sir," I say but I didn't hear one word he said. My whole body is still shaking.

"If you are in trouble or if you or Abigail or your mama needs help, there is nowhere else I'd rather be than right here talking to you. Okay?"

"Yes sir."

"Are you in trouble?"

"Not right now, but the day is young," I say, thinking quick.

He smiles and touches me on the top of the head. "Fair enough. Can you get your daddy for me? I need to talk to him about this letter."

I turn and run to get back up onto the porch and holler. Daddy rolls out from under the truck and wipes his hands, slamming the radio off. "What say, Dale?"

"Hey, Jackson. That Sammy Cotter's truck?"

"Sure the hell is. I don't keep Toyota parts so I'm waiting for a Jap-box."

"I hear ya, man." Officer Overton walks slow toward the garage. "I'm sorry about what happened to Sarah. I wish I had been at the wreck to help out. Where was it?"

Daddy pointed toward town. "Freemont and Thigpen."

"I was on duty and it didn't even come up on my pager."

Daddy stuffs his rag into his pocket and walks slow toward Officer Overton. I rub my hands over the wood of the porch, watching them.

"Huh," Daddy says, tilting his head.

Officer Overton says, "But the radios can be buggy."

"Well, it didn't call for a fuss. I threw her in my truck and took her in myself."

"You really should call us if something like that happens. It could've been a lot worse."

"She'll get over it."

"I'm not sure about that. I went to the hospital this morning to talk to her doctors and get a statement from her."

The air between them changes from summer to winter with just a few words. Daddy stops walking. The two of them look at each other for a long time.

"Emma, can you go in the house for me?" Officer Overton says, all nice.

"She can stay if she wants," Daddy says, mean.

I run inside.

Loretta needs me to put her out of her suffering. That is something I can do, instead of just waiting here in this house all by myself while everything happens around me like a tornado. Daddy's Beretta is under he and Abigail's bed, empty with a box of bullets next to it. I stuff my pockets to be sure and go out the back door. The trees are all orange and yellow and red around me and the ground is covered with leaves and it looks like the world is on fire.

Once I am in the woods I pull the clip out of the gun and rack the slide. I don't want to have to shoot Loretta but putting her out of her suffering is the kind thing to do so she will not be in pain and scared anymore. I got a certificate for kindness from Ms. Atkins because London Barnes who is named after a city got her hair caught in a fire extinguisher on the wall and I helped pull it out so that is how I know I am a kind person.

My body is as scared as it's ever been but my brain is saying pop it in the head, pop it in the head, pop it in the head while my heart slams against my ribs. When I get there Loretta is lying down in her bed of leaves and whining. My knees shake so bad that I fall down a few feet away from her the same way my sister fell down in church yesterday.

"Loretta." I am crying. "My daddy loves me, and Abigail, and my mama, okay? But he loves you best, okay?"

I look at my daddy's dog, stand up, and make my stance real careful. I take aim at her shoulder but my hands are shaking so bad that I'm scared I will miss. I don't want to hurt her or anything else, even though I am sure it's too late to do enough good things to get back on God's good side if shooting a dog is a good thing at all.

It is hard. I try counting to three, but my finger is frozen on the trigger because killing a dog does not feel like shooting a wooden target. I try counting down from three. Then I try counting from one to ten and then from ten down to one. I try staring right at her and I try closing my eyes. I try aiming at her eyeball and I try aiming at her nose. I try imagining how happy Loretta will be when she wakes up in Heaven where everything is perfect forever and she will think about how nice it was for Emma to put her out of her suffering like that. But it is too hard.

I put the gun into the waistband of my pants and kneel down and peel the rope out of the bloody places on her neck. It takes me a minute of working but I get the knot loose and help her up. She runs away from me and away from our house and I don't blame her and it is not long before I can't see her anymore.

The gun gets heavy in my hand. Everything is heavy. My body is too heavy for me to hold up so I lean against the tree with the rope still wrapped around it. There are chiggers on my arm now and the wind tickles the leaves in the trees so that there is noise everywhere and I cannot stand the noise anymore and little sparkles of sun come down and I cannot stand the light. My daddy is hollering way off on the other side of the woods, something about how he has the right. Then there is one blip of Officer Overton's police siren and I can hear the sound of an engine revving and pulling out down the road toward town.

Then my daddy calls my name. He is standing on the porch

it sounds like, angry as a hornet at the world and I do not even have Loretta to make him feel better. I imagine what his face must look like because he is realizing right now that Mama, Abigail, and his dog are all gone and I am the only one he has left to feed him and wash his clothes and sleep with him in his bed. His cheeks and forehead are probably bright red and his hands will be harder than hammers on me until the day I die and only then will it all stop. It will all stop.

There is a blue jay sitting on a branch a few trees away from me and in the morning sun it is the prettiest blue I've ever seen in my life, prettier than any paint or crayon or marker could ever be. When my daddy calls my name again that pretty blue bird gets scared and flies up up and away. I watch until it's gone and then I take a deep breath and hold it hard in my chest like I am hugging the air itself. I lift my daddy's Beretta 92 and take aim but I don't bother hitting my stance because I know I will not miss.

LEAD US NOT

IT WAS MITCHELL CANTER'S SIXTY-FIFTH birthday. When he woke up, his wife Dora asked if he wanted her to go to the store later to get a carrot cake.

"Gotta watch my blood sugar."

Dora groaned as she rolled over to pat his back. "I'll get cupcakes," she said. "They got that bakery shelf in the store, now. You know, you can get just one or two cupcakes, little things, if there's not a big to-do. Sometimes I walk by there and feel like I want something for myself for no reason at all."

"You need to watch your sugar, too."

"Well, gotta have cake on a birthday."

He stretched his arms up with a grunt. "Well, now, I reckon I can agree with that."

Mitchell knew she wanted the cake more than she wanted him to have the cake, but that was fine by him. At this point in their marriage, most things were fine by him.

He pulled on a pair of jeans and buttoned a flannel over his sleep shirt. "I'm going to go get some breakfast."

"Bring me something back for lunch."

"I will."

When he got down the road and crossed the bridge over the pond, Mitchell's fingers were already stiff with cold on the steering wheel, and his creaky shoulder was hard to move when he lifted his hand to wave at Jackson Hatcher's trailer without bothering to look up. The mechanic was usually outside on his porch smoking around this time, so it had become their tradition to greet one another in this small way every morning.

Dora called the entire Hatcher family white trash, but their little ragamuffin girl was cute enough. Poked her lip out to anyone at Austin's Grill who would feel sorry enough to buy her a grilled cheese. Mitchell had probably bought her five or six just in the last year. He knew Jackson took care of his girls and woman but that little girl always had a way of looking pretty hungry all the time. Good kid.

Austin's Grill had biscuits, breakfast food, burgers, hot dogs, and grilled cheese. No other restaurant survived in Bethany because Bethany didn't need another restaurant. The afternoons were for stay-at-home mothers, baseball teams, farmers, construction workers, and folks from the city looking for "good old Southern food" only to turn back around in the doorway with nervous smiles when they saw all the grease.

Austin unlocked the doors at half past five every morning specifically for the local patriarchs: Johnny Barnes, Roy Freedman, Samuel Cotter, and Mitchell, who was turning sixty-five today. They sat together every morning at a round table affectionately referred to by the town as the Table of Knowledge. Truth be told, there was not much special about this birthday, as this was exactly what he did yesterday, and the day before, and on his birthday for the last ten years.

Johnny Barnes was already there, clearing his old smoker's throat behind his newspaper when Mitchell walked in.

"What say, Mitch?" Johnny said.

"Well, it's my birthday. Sixty-five."

"Oh I hear you, man. I ain't getting any younger either." Johnny flicked his newspaper, and Mitchell took his coat off and sat down.

Austin brought Mitch his coffee and reminded him that Dora told him to make sure he used the pink sugar instead of the white. Mitch decided to be cute about it. "Aww, but it's my birthday!"

"Your diabetes don't know that," Austin responded and walked back around the counter to throw some frozen sausage patties onto the old black griddle.

Sammy Cotter's truck—with the broken dryer still in the back as it had been for two weeks—was the next one to pull into the dirt lot right in front of the door. Sammy Cotter was allowed to have white sugar, but not sausage or pancakes.

"What say, Johnny, Mitch?" he said over the sound of the clanging Christmas bells on the back of the door that stayed up all year.

Mitch said, "Not much. It's my birthday."

"Well, I still ain't fixed that damn dryer." Sammy plopped slowly and unceremoniously into his usual spot with a groan. "And I think today's the day Emily's finally gonna kill me over it."

Johnny huffed disapprovingly. "She's always in a fit about something. I'm telling you, Sammy, for all she goes to church on Sunday, you need to tell her that wives are supposed to submit to their husbands. The way she talks to you ain't right. That's Genesis."

"Well, you can go tell her that, if you want. Won't fix the damn dryer."

Roy Freedman came in next, puffing warm air into his hands. "Morning, boys."

"Morning, Roy."

"NPR was a damn mess this morning."

"Now, why the hell do you listen to it if it's only gonna make you mad?" Sammy asked, for the hundredth time.

"I like the commercials. What say, Mitch?"

"It's my birthday."

"Oh," Roy said, solemnly. He patted Mitchell's shoulder and sat down in the last remaining chair. "I know I'm gonna need some strong coffee to deal with what the Democrats in the House did yesterday."

"I'm sure you'll tell us all about it," Johnny said, folding his newspaper so the daily crossword was all he could see.

They no longer had to wait for Floyd Underwood, who was always late, because he'd passed a few years back. Jesus, had it been that long? So now that all were present, they partook in their various first courses, a humble array of eggs and sausage and bacon and biscuits and grits so buttered that they were actually yellow. Mitchell wanted molasses on his biscuit, but Austin said no again. It's not a free country when your wife, God bless her, keeps tabs on you even when she's asleep. Good woman.

Sergeant Simmons came in at a quarter past six, looking exhausted.

"What say, Sims?" Roy asked. "What's the news this fine morning?"

"Shew," is all the man said, drawing the word out bitterly and shaking his head.

"Oh, I hear ya," Mitchell attempted. "It's my birthday. Sixty-five."

The sergeant took his hat off to rub his cold, balding head. He looked weary, and his voice was hoarse. "We found Jackson Hatcher's little girl dead in the damn woods by Coolie's Pond last night."

Johnny looked up from his crossword suddenly, and Roy put his coffee down. In the quiet of the tiny diner, Austin nearly dropped the Tropicana pulp-free he was pouring for himself. No one said anything until Mitchell whispered, ". . . damn."

"What the hell happened?"

"Shot right in the head."

"Lord have mercy," Johnny muttered.

"Get popped by a hunter?"

"Don't know yet. But you know Jackson's wife got in that car accident last week and just died at the hospital, and his older girl's gone missing, and now his little girl's at the funeral home."

Roy looked absolutely confused; for all of his time dabbling in specific niches of politics, actual human suffering rarely came into the discussions he listened to. Mitchell didn't know what to think either. He felt like he'd just seen Jackson's wife Sarah a few days ago, but hell, everything felt that way to him now.

"Jackson was just working on my truck the other day," Sammy said.

The sergeant shook his head wearily. "Damn fucking mess, excuse my language."

"Ain't no kids in here," Austin said quietly from behind the counter, dumping a big bag of ice into the back of the Coke machine, probably trying to figure out the last time he'd seen the little Hatcher girl. "Say what you want. Hard night."

"Dale'll straighten it all out," Roy finally said with a nod.

The young officer had grown up in Bethany, so he must have grown up right. Good guy. "He's got an eye for this sort of thing."

"Ain't nothing like *this sort of thing* ever happened here," Sammy muttered.

"Well poor Dale's the one that found her," Simmons said. "He's a wreck."

"Jesus Christ," Sammy said, rubbing his eye roughly like there was something in it. Austin put a piece of sausage and a slice of orange American cheese and some egg on a biscuit, and gave it to Simmons, waving off the five dollar bill and shaking his head.

"Go on home and get you some rest."

"Reckon I will. You boys stay out of trouble."

The little joke fell flat today. The happy Christmas bells sounded mournful when Simmon's left, and Johnny shook his head. "I know Samantha will want to do something for Jackson. Damn, it's like something straight out of Job. I can't imagine."

"She was a sweet kid."

The other men grunted their affirmation, but the truth of the matter was that she was really not a sweet kid at all. She was a clever kid, a cute kid, a mischievous kid, but sweet was not the word anyone would use to honestly describe her. She was the town urchin. She frightened her Sunday school teachers and bullied her classmates and then had the gall to bring her scrawny rear to Austin's to mope around for food all afternoon. Johnny swore up and down that he saw her snatch a ten out of the collection plate one Sunday, and Sammy's grandson—a football player—had come home from a field day with a busted cheek from a rock he said Emma Hatcher threw. Good arm, at least.

"Sweet kid," Sammy muttered again.

Johnny looked back down at his crossword puzzle but spent

a few minutes just tapping the eraser of his worn little pencil against the table.

"A hunter got her," Roy said after looking out of the window for a while. "Thought she was a deer. Guarantee it. Just didn't see her until it was too late."

Mitchell spent the next hour or so nursing his coffee, running his finger along the broken parts of the old mug, and looking at the worn, plastic fly swatter on the wall hanging from a nail that Sammy had put in himself. They used it in the summer to smack flies off of the table. Mitchell thought about his own grown kids, one living next door with two babies of her own and the other working on his second degree in the city. He wondered what it was in a person that made them stay here, and what it was that made someone leave—a gene or an instinct, nature versus nurture. He did not want a cupcake anymore. He wanted an entire cake.

"Five-letter word for a purse or bag, boys," Johnny said.

Roy swallowed a bite of biscuit. "Purse is a five-letter word."

"Purse is the clue, though."

"Does purse fit in the boxes?" Mitchell asked.

"Nah, there's already an 'H' in there."

Kaisleigh Johnson, who had moved here for the small-town charm from up north somewhere, came in with the loud rattling of the bells, then snuck up behind the men and squealed to announce her presence. She patted Sammy's shoulder like they'd known each other for years.

Roy turned his head away and made a face. Kaisleigh always smelled like a perfume store.

"Mr. Sammy, you are *still* working on that lawn mower, huh?"

"Sure am."

"Oh, don't we all know it? It's been hanging up from the

swingset for a few months, now. I'm surprised those chains haven't rusted clean off it."

"Well I can't get under it if it ain't in the air," he said dryly.

She laughed and flicked her neat bangs. "Well, on an unrelated topic, we talked in the home owners committee meeting about keeping yards clean so they don't drive down the value of the houses going up in the new subdivision."

"That seems related to me," Mitchell pointed out.

"Well, a few of the other ladies there made good points. I don't know, though. I'm on the fence about it. Get it? On the fence."

"What?" Sammy asked. "Your fence is broken too." He sat up straight in his chair. "Well, now, I ain't joined no damn home-owner club but if one of them ladies wants to come clean my yard, they're welcome to."

"Oh, no, honey. You know I like to keep things tidy, but I'd never tell anyone what to do in their yard," she laughed. "But I love what Mr. Johnny does with his bushes. They're always so trim and nice-looking."

"I keep 'em cut in the shape of the four creatures John saw on Patmos in Revelation," Johnny said, only barely looking up from his crossword puzzle.

Roy, who was in the middle of drinking coffee, snorted into his mug.

Kaisleigh hesitated for a moment. "Well, that's . . . sweet."

"What's a five-letter word for purse or bag?" Johnny said, doing her the favor of changing the subject.

"Clutch!"

He started writing the letters in, then paused, rolled his eyes, and flipped the pencil to erase them.

Austin called Kaisleigh's name and passed her the bag of

biscuits she usually picked up for her four blonde, beautiful kids. "Y'all take care!" she winked.

Roy, always the most friendly of the group, waved as she left.

"Don't let the damn door hit you," Sammy said under his breath. "She needs to go the hell back to wherever she came from."

"Don't she have a kid named Journey?" Mitchell asked.

"J-U-R-N-E-E," Johnny said. "Yeah."

"I swear, she's near 'bout the whitest person I've ever met in my life," Roy said.

Mitchell's little alarm went off at eight, indicating it was time for him to take the four pills in the ziplock bag in his coat pocket. As usual, this prompted Roy and Sammy to take theirs as well, which prompted all of them to wave Austin down for their second course of the morning; those who had eaten well an hour earlier, ate smaller. Those who had eaten small, ate grander. And at a quarter past eight, the infamous Nettie Coats walked in with a distinct whiff of goats and an annoyed click of her tongue at the jangling bells hanging on the back of the door. She never was one for Christmas decorations in October.

Roy had always been sweet on her, despite her giving absolutely no sign that she had any interest in any man after her husband left her a year or two prior. He was a few decades her senior anyway, but they all liked her; she had a spunk and wit that their wives—God bless them—sorely lacked. Good woman.

"What say, Nettie Coats?" Roy asked, looking up from his paper.

"Y'all heard about the fucking Hatchers?" she asked immediately, using a pocket-knife to clean under her farm-worn nails.

"Simmons came in this morning," Mitchell said. "Can't believe Jackson's bad luck."

"Oh, is that what folks are calling it?" she asked.

"You want something for your boy this morning, Nettie?" Austin asked. He grabbed a bag of Wonder bread off a shelf from under the counter.

"That'd be good, thanks." Nettie dropped her Carhartt on the back of a chair and sat down at the next table. No one had seen her son in years. He didn't get out much, which was a source of good, wholesome conversation around town. He had, quotation fingers, problems. He was always real quiet. Not a big talker, not too bright. Some said he lived in a eight by ten room above Nettie's barn and slept on a blow-up mattress. Others said he lived in the basement. Mitchell couldn't understand why folks thought he wouldn't stay in his own damn room if he was still living at home.

Johnny looked up from his crossword. "Nettie-girl, what's a six-letter word for a conundrum?"

"Oh, fuck if I know, Johnny. I do jigsaw puzzles."

"What is it if it ain't bad luck?" Mitchell finally asked.

Nettie raised her eyebrow. "Divine punishment if God has any say in it. Jackson's a damn snake. You know he was beating on his wife and doing who-knows-what to those girls."

"Oh, I don't know about all that," Mitchell said. "I like Jackson all right."

"Have you ever met him?" Nettie asked.

"Well, now, I don't like to speculate," Roy said, ". . . but I never liked him. He curses in front of ladies."

Nettie made a *pft* noise.

"You think he was whooping on the girls?" Mitchell wondered.

"Kids need whoopings," Johnny said. "Especially these days. They've got no respect."

"Whoopings is one thing, but his oldest ran off, and Dale found Jackson's Beretta on the ground by that poor girl," Nettie said.

"Dale found what, now?" Sammy asked.

"You heard me."

"Bad ears," Roy said, drawing a circle with his finger beside his head.

Nettie leaned forward and enunciated each word much louder, "That little girl blew her brains out."

"Lord have mercy, Nettie, hush," Austin barked, nodding toward the other customers.

After a moment of stunned silence, Sammy shook his head and tutted. "Well, Emma always was a little touched in the head." Then he looked at Nettie. "No offense."

"Touched in the head is one thing, but she's what, six? Seven?" Johnny asked. "Little young to be that messed up, isn't it?"

"Eight," Nettie said. "And, you know, I don't want even want to know what would make an eight-year-old fucking blow her brains out in the woods."

"Touched," Johnny said, quietly. "That's what it was."

Because saying literally anything else would imply they thought Jackson was guilty of something, and a real man would never be guilty of anything like that. Jackson was a hard worker, spent his days under cars. The Hatchers didn't have a great life, but they stayed fed, and had raggedy clothes on their backs. Jackson smoked and liked his beer, but so did everyone else. He was a real man, all right. A good man. He was just a real unlucky good man.

Johnny looked back down at his crossword but wasn't too interested in conundrum anymore. Nettie kept cleaning out her nails, wiping the dirt on her pants, cool as you please but obviously seething underneath it all.

Sammy finally piped up. "Y'know, just seems like more kids are messed up now than they were in our day. Kids just weren't that messed up when we were growing up. Now it seems like every other kid's got something going on in the head. I grew up with lawn darts and Vietnam and lead paint, and I turned out all right. Kids now are just damn . . . fragile."

"No God in the schools," Johnny said. "We're paying for it."

"Liberals," Roy chimed in. "That's what it is."

Austin hung over the counter to hand Nettie her bag and a styrofoam cup of tea. She handed him a ten dollar bill. "Keep it, Austin."

"Thank ya, ma'am."

She pulled out her own biscuit and took a big bite right as Pastor Ryan walked in at half past eight. Then she promptly started wrapping it back up, but not promptly enough. "Oh, shit."

"Well, hello, stranger!"

Nettie turned and tried to smile, but it looked as forced as it obviously felt. "Oops, sorry preacher, but you just missed me. I was just about to walk out."

"I'll tell you where we miss you, and that's in church."

"I'll be there as soon as you get your DJ to play some Dolly Parton," she said, gathering her things. It was impossible to tell by her tone and facial expression whether or not she was being serious. Mitchell tried to hide his smile. "You can't have church without Dolly."

"You take it easy, Nettie," Roy said, chuckling under his breath.

"She's the songbird of the South!" Nettie announced over

her shoulder as she hustled out the door, leaving the pastor standing there with his jaw agape and the Table of Knowledge laughing to themselves at the mere idea of Nettie Coats attending a church regularly. The Horsemen of the Apocalypse would have to ride, first.

Pastor Ryan was from Franklin County across the state and always insisted on playing Jesus himself in the kids' VBS programs at the church. He and his wife had a garden that produced far too many cucumbers and tomatoes every summer, so she got into the habit of going out before the last hymn and leaving grocery bags full of them on top of everyone's cars. The congregation pretended not to know it was her. They also pretended not to give the cracked, mealy things to their children to throw out the car windows into the woods on the way home. There were only so many cucumber salads and BLTs a household could take.

"Well, what say, Pastor?" Johnny asked. Unlike Nettie, Johnny went to church every Sunday, but spent a good deal of his Monday mornings complaining about the distinct lack of brimstone in Pastor Ryan's preaching. Not enough Old Testament for his liking.

"I'm going to spend the day at the parsonage for those who need to talk about the . . . goings-on."

"It's not on us to pry," Roy said, politely. "But do you have any idea what's going on?"

Pastor Ryan cleared his throat. "Well, you know Sarah got into that car accident up on Thigpen. They got her to the hospital, but she went home to be with her Lord."

"They must've done a good job cleaning it up," Sammy said. "I live at that intersection and never heard a thing."

Johnny looked up at Mitchell, but neither of them said anything.

"Well you know his little one was always a bit off. Troubled.

She killed herself out in the woods, but now it looks like the coroner's found some kind of abuse on her, or something like that."

"What kind of abuse?"

"The . . . inappropriate kind."

Roy tilted his head, confused, like his aging mind was having trouble understanding what kinds of abuse were appropriate. It was like someone walked in and dumped a hundred gigantic puzzle pieces on the Table of Knowledge, and none of them fit together.

"Well, Jackson never'd let anyone put a hand on those girls," Mitchell decided to say. "I know he's torn slam up."

"We all are. It's an unholy mess. And now his oldest one's done run off."

"Well now, she was always quiet, too," Sammy said.

Pastor Ryan pulled a seat and sat backward in it. Johnny looked offended. Some things men just shouldn't do and sitting backward in a chair was one of them.

"I'm doing a grief counseling program after church this coming Sunday for anyone's having trouble understanding all this. The Bible has a lot to say to us about grief. You know the shortest verse in the Bible?"

"He wept," Johnny answered, doodling idly on the corner of his newspaper.

"Bingo! He wept. So we're all just gonna pray for Jackson, and for God to lead him and us through this valley and out to the other side."

Johnny looked up at the ceiling thoughtfully. Religion was his area and he still didn't have anything to say.

Mitchell looked at Sammy, who shrugged and shook his head, defeated.

"Amen, I suppose," Roy finally said.

Business at Austin's picked up with a sudden rush at about nine, as usual; this was normally about the time that Bethany started waking up in earnest. Thankfully, the pastor went home shortly thereafter to put together his grief curriculum, which the men at the Table supposed was probably a needlessly complicated business. Mitchell thought that counseling was done by folks with education, but maybe you didn't need an education to explain the Hatchers. Maybe you just needed a great deal of emotional fortitude.

No one else talked to the old men about it directly, and while they did not normally make it a point to eavesdrop on the loud chatter of the diner at mid-morning—because they normally didn't care about any of Bethany's various dramas or crises—every time someone muttered the name "Hatcher," one of them would cock their head, prompting the others to look up and do the same.

But no one else seemed to know any more than they did, and most knew even less, which was usually the state of things. Officer Dale Overton's mother came in to get breakfast for herself and her son, but said nothing to anyone, and her face was unreadable.

But Tommy Hawthorne got rid of a wasp nest in the crawlspace of his garage with a Shop Vac. Sucked it right on up and only got stung three times, thank God. Then Roy told them all again how he had stepped in a yellow jacket hole a few weeks ago and got stung near 'bout to death. Sammy's grandson was all dressed up for football practice when he came in for breakfast and stood with his hip pressed to Sammy's shoulder so the old man could pat his back and give his usual speech about how fast he could run, like a bullet. He was going to be a fine receiver and play for the university one day. The other men nodded in agreement, and then Sammy looked at his daughter and said, "They ought not be wearing them digging shoes in here. Scuffing up Austin's floor." She just kissed his forehead and patted his shoulder.

Mitchell waved down another coffee, and Johnny put his crossword under his elbow as it rested on the table. They all fell quiet as they watched the crowd flowing in and ebbing back out. Some people stopped by the Table to pay their respects and talk, but most just went straight to the counter and then straight out the door, which was fine by them.

Mitchell finally cleared his throat and looked at Johnny. "You tell Samantha to call Dora, see if they want to cook a little bit for Jackson."

"I'll do that."

"I'll ask Emily," Sammy said. "Hopefully all of this mess will get her mind off the dryer. I don't have time to fix it. Too busy." He polished off his coffee from the sage-green mug.

At quarter past eleven, the Table of Knowledge broke apart with some fond, grumbled farewells. The patriarchs returned to their lives, for the next eighteen hours anyway: Johnny Barnes, who owned a Bible that did not have all of the answers; Roy Freedman, who paid a lot of attention to a government that didn't give two shits about dead little girls in the woods; Samuel Cotter, whose wife would nevertheless complain about the dryer again when he got home, and Mitchell Canter, who turned sixty-five today.

They'd all see each other tomorrow.

DELIVER US

IT WAS ALMOST WINTER WHEN Charlotte Overton came back to town. Her husband, Officer Dale Overton, had been enjoying a brief stay in a psyche ward when she ran off and found the only person in the nearest city with a spare bed—a goofy, existentialist drug dealer named Stephen. Dale hated Stephen's faux-profound attitude when they were all kids in Bethany, so Charlie knew she'd be safe there. And she was.

It took a lot of convincing for Stephen to accept the arrangement living with a police officer's good young Christian wife, but she proved that she didn't have to make the deals or handle the accounts directly to be useful. Her nose was much sharper than his, for one; she could more easily tell the difference between white widow and sour diesel. She counted tiny yellow pills, watered the plants under the blue lights in the closet, weighed baggies, and made sure all the twenties were facing the same way before they went into the cookie tin with "To Stevie, from Grandma" written on a Santa Clause gift sticker on the front. He paid her with a room, some anxiety meds (which she had never needed until Dale's mental state started going south), and decent extramarital sex a few times a week. She talked to her family very little during this time and didn't speak to her husband at all.

She dreamt about her wedding day, though, with an empty space at the altar beside her. The knowledge that she did not remember what her husband was like before the rage attacks and cursing and unabating depression haunted her like the memory of the night she threw him out, and when sleeping with her guilt became more unbearable than living with it, Charlie left Stephen's and moved back in with her parents in Bethany just weeks after the Great Jackson Hatcher Incident, until she could determine just how irreparable the damage to her marriage really was.

Nettie Coats had an ad in the paper for a part-time "Marketing Associate," which Charlie understood as sitting behind the table at the farmers market. Nettie had always harbored a soft spot for Charlie and easily agreed to hire her. After what she did to Dale, Charlie felt like a perpetual fugitive, powerlessly indebted to the shelter of others.

Charlie pulled into the dirt parking lot at seven sharp for her second weekend shift at the farmers market, with her sunglasses on and her hood up so she wouldn't need to make eye contact with anyone. No one who lived in Bethany actually bought anything here. They shopped at the local Food Lion, except for the Real Housewives over in the subdivision who made the trip to Harris Teeter a few exits down the highway for Greek yogurt and chia seeds and Venezuelan coffee they could grind themselves. But the tourists from out of town liked the market, and they came in droves every weekend with "Buy Local" bumper-stickers and more money than they obviously had the sense to know what to do with.

Nettie was rubbing her aged, dirt-worn hands by the heater in the tent when Charlie walked up and handed her a sausage biscuit wrapped in tin foil from Austin's Grill.

During the summer, the Coats' farm tent sold giant jars of dark-brown clover honey, homemade breads and cakes, zucchini and cucumbers big as Charlie's forearm, potatoes and onions by the sack, and tomatoes so juicy that the skins cracked and split and leaked in the sun. In the winter, collards. Thick, wet bundles of gray collards, stacked three feet high on the table and held together with giant blue rubber bands, the leaves pocked with flea-beetle holes.

Nettie offered Charlie the open end of a pack of Mistys. "Get your smokes out before the customers get here," she instructed sagely. Nettie seemed to enjoy being the Yoda of produce, and having someone to talk to. "You going to the ceremony next week?" she asked.

"Are you?" Charlie responded, clicking her lighter.

"It's my stinking garage, now that Earl's gone. I reckon I'll have to."

"Is Ethan?"

"I doubt he'd leave the basement after all these years just to honor the asshole that ran out on us."

Charlie couldn't tell what was smoke and what was steam against the air when she exhaled. Most of the town felt obligated to excuse Nettie's irreverent abrasiveness because she was a mother with a dead son. Her ex-husband, however, was a different story. He'd been hated by everyone but Nettie from the beginning. Earl Coats of Earl's Auto Services & Supply used to charge too much for labor and double what he should have for parts, paid his mechanics less than half of what he earned, and profited handsomely from the slow destruction of many a good, reliable Chevy in town. Earl was probably the second most-hated man in Bethany, after Jackson Hatcher, who killed his wife, ran his oldest daughter off to God-knows-where, and drove his youngest to kill herself a few weeks ago. It was hard to top that.

Nettie and her husband had been each other's favorite kind of asshole. They made one another happy enough for many years, but once Gentry died, something snapped in their relationship. After that, they got on like a burning house. Their surviving son Ethan had all sorts of rumors circulating the town about him—how he had a mental breakdown after finding Gentry's dead body, how Earl leaving made things even worse, how he'd grown morbidly obese and disappeared into the basement of their home like a troll and never came back out again.

January was a boring time to work the farmers market. The New Years Resolution bunch came out in packs from the city, woven baskets and paleo recipes in hand, expecting tomatoes and peppers and radishes and seeing nothing but greens. They usually bought an obligatory bunch of collards out of politeness, which was the only reason anyone out there made any money. "Don't y'all forget to wash those again when they're half done," Charlie called cheerfully to one couple as they walked away, disappointed.

"Fucking morons," Nettie said. "I couldn't afford to wipe my ass if Ethan wasn't paying rent."

"How does he have a job if he never leaves the basement?" Charlie asked.

"Something on the computer," she said. "He's arachnophobic, you know."

Charlie had to fight not to laugh. "I think you mean agoraphobic, Nettie. Is he on anything?"

"Can't go to the doctor."

"Was he ever on anything?" Charlie wanted to see if it was something she recognized from her time with Stephen.

"Kl-something." Nettie pointed at the couple with the lit end of her cigarette as they got into their car. "You know what I hate most about people like them? First thing they always wanna know is, they'll ask you"—she flopped her hands like a seal—"'Is this organic?' And you know, I didn't even know what that meant for the longest time. Do you know what it means?"

"Don't think I do."

"Means is your stock grown in shit. That's what they want to know. And let me tell you right here and now, I don't grow my garden in shit. I grow my garden with TrueGreen phosphorous fertilizer from the hardware store like a normal person."

"Well, what do you say when people ask?"

"I tell 'em it's my own shit I grow it in."

Charlie barely got a laugh out before she saw a police car and her whole body froze, heart plummeting in her chest and beating *no, no, not yet, not yet, not ready.* She fished in her pocket for a yellow pill, put it under her tongue, then sank deeper into her jacket and tried to make out the shape of the face inside the tinted window. By the time the bitter pill turned to chalk in her mouth, her husband Dale had climbed out of the car and walked across the square, vigorously shaking hands with a few men nearby, laughing, barrel-chested in his uniform. It was the first time Charlie had seen him since the night he threw the plate of spaghetti at her head, the night she'd thrown him out of the house. He'd gotten big from whatever medications he was on, but other than that, he looked pretty normal.

When Dale turned in her direction, she snatched the cigarette out of her own mouth and threw it into the grass. He kept walking, showing no sign that he'd actually seen her.

"He knows you're back," Nettie said, amused.

"How do you know?"

"It's not a big town, honey." She laughed a little. "And he's all over the place lately, talking up *his* new fire station. He's very proud to be taking that garage off my hands to convert it. The whole thing is his pride and joy."

Charlie knew him well enough to know that he was compensating. "Well, we always wanted kids. I guess a fire station is the best he's gonna get for now."

They had five customers from sunrise to noon, and sold twenty-three dollars worth of collards.

"You're getting too old to be out here all day," Charlie said.

"Fuck you."

"Go home. I'll bring everything to your place when I'm done."

"Yeah, all right." Nettie stood up with a few pops and a groan, then pulled a ratty ball cap over her thinning hair. "Ethan would probably like to see you," she said.

"Does he like visitors?"

"Hell if I know. He's never had one."

Once Nettie left, Charlie got busy smoking the other half of her pack of cigarettes, listening to music on her phone, and plucking the brown leaves off of the bunches of collards on the table to pass the time. She didn't have any more customers and Dale was nowhere to be seen after his initial walk around the market.

It took about a half-hour to pack everything up. It was hard to wrangle the folding tables and the heavy collapsible tent by herself, and while a few people walked by and grunted greetings, no one offered to help. Occasionally she felt the back of her neck prickling, and turned around to catch a cluster of people staring in her direction. She'd spent years of her life quietly resenting living life in Dale's shadow, but now Charlie would've given anything to make the town forget her name entirely.

When she stopped by her parents' split-level off of Pine Street, her father was cursing at the television in his armchair, hitting a homemade Manhattan pretty hard for a Saturday afternoon. He had the hiccups. The whites of his eyes had turned yellow at some point during her yearlong absence. Charlie touched his shoulder on her way in and he kissed her hand. "There's my girl. Hey, darling. Hic." It caused her insides to twist up in agony when she remembered there would be a time—perhaps soon—when she would not have him anymore.

Her mother, on the other hand, was a sweet, church-going, knitting, retired nurse who hadn't touched a drop of alcohol in twenty years, no-sir-not-a-drop, except for the glass of Pinot she drank every night before bed to compliment her Ambien. She loved Dale like a son, still. Charlie didn't have the heart to tell anyone the gory details of what she'd suffered at his hands—his yelling and weeping over Gentry, his days without sleep, his paranoia, his rage—and Charlie doubted anyone would believe her if she did.

Her mother was washing dishes when Charlie put the collards on the counter. "Did you see Dale today?" she asked, like she had every day for the past week.

"No," Charlie said, not quite dishonestly.

His praise started rolling from her mother's mouth. She took him food when he was on duty at the fire station, stood next to him when he sang tenor in the church choir, and had him over for dinner regularly. "He worked the volunteer shift last Christmas to give the boys a chance to be with their families. Sweet thing."

That Christmas Eve, Charlie was worlds away, listening to Stephen take an after-sex shower while she shoved every one of the unmarked bottles of anxiety pills into a knapsack. She needed them more than he needed the money he'd make selling them. Charlie dragged three trash bags that she'd stuffed with her clothes that morning out of the closet, and yelled over her shoulder that she wanted to spend the holiday with her folks, whom he'd never met despite also originating from Bethany, and that she loved him, which wasn't even close to being true. Charlie took his last can of Bud Light and ran toward the truck that she and Dale bought together, bags slung across her back. She reminded herself of the old Grinch cartoon she used to watch every Christmas.

Her mother shook water over the greens Charlie'd brought, talking about how good of an idea it was for Dale to convince the town council to buy the garage from Nettie and turn it into the second fire station, because that nasty old building was too visible to be that much of an eyesore—"I swear it's been turning off the tourists"—and how much money Nettie would get, and how thankful Nettie and the rest of the town should be toward Dale. "Nettie's full of vinegar toward him, still, but she should be grateful to him for coming up with it. We should all be grateful to him. Especially you, Honeybear."

"Me?" Charlie asked. "Why?"

"He's got every right to be upset with you, but he's not. Tells anyone who brings you up that he misses you and wants things to work out. He's a good man."

"Shit," her father dropped his glass a little too hard on the table. "I wish you'd shut up and leave her alone," he yelled from the living room. "Why don't *you* go marry the boy so *you* can watch the sun rise out of his ass every morning?"

Charlie put her hand over her mouth to hide her laughter. Her mother ignored him like she usually did. "Are you going to the ceremony next week?" her mother asked, snapping stems. "The choir is singing. I know he'd appreciate you being there."

"I don't think anyone there would want to see me," Charlie said, standing up and going to the refrigerator to prod at the photographs and Christmas cards and sticky notes and old shopping lists. She and Dale smiled out from under a recipe for strawberry cake clipped out of a magazine. They were walking out of the church fellowship hall through a veil of bubbles on their wedding day. Charlie recalled the feeling of climbing into the truck with him to go back to the home they already shared, packing for a cheap honeymoon at the beach they visited every summer, him bear-hugging her from behind when she wasn't expecting it. They were a walking, talking country love song. She remembered the way the sun teased off the insignia on his Air Force uniform when they posed in front of the azaleas for wedding photos.

He was it. He was the *Good Man*. He was a police officer on his working days and a volunteer firefighter in his spare time and he'd get out of bed to pull someone out of the ditch at three in the morning and mow an old lady's lawn just because—and he was hers. She used to beam with pride when people told her, "You landed a good one. You're a lucky gal." Now, she remembered those words with shame and resentment. No one, to her knowledge, had ever clapped his shoulder and told him that *he* was lucky to have *her*. Because he wasn't.

She needed a resolution. Any kind of resolution. At this

point, she'd be just as happy with him backhanding her in the town square with divorce papers as she would be trying to work it out and save their marriage.

Charlie pulled the recipe over the photograph to hide it and snatched the refrigerator door open, grabbing a Pepsi. She pointed at the collards in the sink. "Wash those twice," she said to her mother.

"Are you coming home for dinner?"

"Probably," Charlie answered.

"Want me to invite Dale?"

"Mom."

On the way out of the house, her father caught her hand from his armchair and squeezed it. "I love you," Charlie said.

"It's good to have you home, Sweet Pea," he muttered, with the smallest of slurs. "*I'm* glad to have you home. It's hard work living with an angel." He jerked his head at the kitchen. "It'll give you a complex after a while, you know?"

She told him she did know.

Charlie and Ethan had dated in middle school, if "dated" was the word for studying science flash cards on the bus and occasionally holding hands. When she tried to envision what he might look like now, she kept imagining Quasimodo shrinking away from the sun and the eyes of the public. Charlie understood what it meant to be so heavy with shame and grief that the only place to go was out of sight.

When she arrived at the Coats' farm, Charlie honked to announce her presence, left her truck beside Nettie's, then walked down the hill toward the back of the farmhouse. Rogue boxwood branches reached and grasped one another over the small stoop in front of the basement door; Charlie ducked spider webs and stepped over briars to discover it was locked. There were lights on inside, but blackout curtains blocked her view, so she didn't knock. She wondered what crazed, emaciated zombie lived inside, with long, stringy hair and eyes that blinked in horror at the light of an open window and survived on a diet of hose water and Moon Pies. Charlie wished she'd just made up an excuse when Nettie mentioned her coming to see Ethan, but she had no more excuses left in her. She went back up the hill to the front of the farmhouse and let herself in.

The main foyer was only a few degrees warmer than the outside. Nettie had stuffed folded paper towels into the kitchen windows to keep out the chill. Chips of white paint from the walls and ceilings dusted the surfaces below. To say the place needed a masculine touch—or any touch, really—was putting it lightly. Gray smoke snaked toward the ceiling from an ashtray beside the chair in the cluttered living room, and on the television, Barney grabbed his belt and leaned back, puffing out his chest in Andy's direction.

Nettie came out of the bathroom, jerked her head "hello," and without another word, flung open the door to the basement. She called downstairs, "Charlie's here to see you."

"Charlie who?"

Charlie hissed, "You didn't tell him I was coming?"

"Charlotte Overton," Nettie yelled.

"Well, good God," Ethan said to himself, just loud enough for them to hear. Nettie turned to Charlie, a look of triumph on her sun-worn face.

"See?" she said. "He's happy." Without another word, she went into the living room and picked up her cigarette, which was still burning. "I'll unload. Take your time."

It happened so fast. Charlie wasn't sure what she was expecting—a chicken leg on a string, some coaxing, a magic flute to soothe the beast. But the voice sounded stable enough. Unsure, but stable.

Standing at the top of the stairs, Charlie recalled the faintest memory of the two of them in seventh grade, waiting after school on the sidewalk for the bus. Ethan had snuck three packs of matches from Gentry's desk drawer in his blue backpack, and he gave Charlie one like a gift. They stood there striking and flicking them across the sidewalk into the bushes, each flame accompanied with the breathless expectation that it would be the one to set the world on fire.

A faint lavender scent from down below drew her feet onto the staircase, a stark contrast to the scent of dirty vegetables behind her.

"Hey, give me a minute," Ethan said. "I'm almost at the end of this hideout."

"No problem," she said nervously, still descending.

"You played Red Dead Redemption yet?"

"I don't watch movies." Charlie stepped onto a black rug at the bottom of the stairs.

"One sec."

The last time Charlie had seen Ethan was at Gentry's funeral. She could barely see the top of his dirty-blonde hair peeking over the back of an office chair. He had his bare feet on the desk, and there was a small camera clipped to the top of the screen in front of him.

"Okay, I'm back, guys. When you clear Twin Rocks, don't forget to go into the house here on the left and—hey, Fox80, welcome—go into the house and open the chest, and you'll get the Volcanic Pistol, which is one of my favorites—see you later, Twisterkins. Now, once you grab that weapon, you can loot some ammo off of the bodies on your way out, but I don't usually waste the time. At this point you should have the money to buy things pretty freely from town."

Charlie stood awkwardly at the bottom of the stairs, not wanting to go wandering around uninvited. Black curtains hung over the door and the tiny basement windows by the ceiling, but pure-white ambient lighting ensured that there were no dark corners in the room. Green bamboo plants and perfectly groomed bonsai trees grew in square vases on every surface, and three or four small humidifiers pumped visible aromatherapy steam into the air. The floor was open concrete, marked with black scuffs from the office chair.

"All right, friends. I'm going to take a break. Grab a snack and hit that Paypal button before the action starts back up. Donors of fifty dollars or more receive pinned shout-outs and cross-pro-motions on my channel for a week. This is GoatsInCoats, sign-ing off. Be back soon."

His fingers clacked for a moment on the keyboard. Charlie counted four computers and three televisions. A counter on the far wall held a mini-fridge, a hotplate, a microwave, and several bags of paper plates and bowls. She could see a bath-room close to the bed, sheet-rocked more recently than the rest of the room.

The space was clean and bright and surprisingly airy, and when Charlie compared it to the dry, rotten, winter-dead world outside, she felt she understood why he refused to come out.

"Hey," Ethan said, spinning around in his office chair.

"Hey yourself," Charlie said. His hair was cropped short on top of his sculpted face. He was wearing a black t-shirt that hugged his chest and pale upper arms in a way that made her wish she'd put on makeup, or shaved her legs, or worn earrings, or something. "Jesus, have you lost weight?"

"Yeah," he said, nodding toward a treadmill. "I've got a pretty solid female fan-base. Guys, too, I guess."

"Well, you look great."

There was a brief silence before he looked around and noticed a dusty cardboard box under a table. "Hey, you want a drink?" he asked, poking at the box and clanking the glass around. She peered over the lip.

"Something brown would be nice," she said.

"It's my dad's old shit, so it'll be good to get rid of it."

"Where'd Earl end up, anyway?" she asked casually, like the fate of his family wasn't inextricably tied with her own.

"Last letter came from Missoula a few years ago." He peeled the wax top off a bottle of Maker's.

"Why don't you just drink it?" she asked.

"Drinking's kind of a social thing, isn't it?" Ethan got himself a bottle of water from his little refrigerator and sat back in his office chair, letting it roll against a desk. Charlie helped herself to a couch. "Heard about you and Dale."

Charlie twisted off the cap of the bourbon. "Yeah."

"No judgment here. Dale was always a little too Captain America for me."

"Well, me taking off on him wasn't so great, either."

"Mom says you ended up outside of Charlotte?"

"Rock Hill."

"What happened?"

"I came back." The impact of the first swig made her body seize.

"Sorry," he said. "It's old."

Footsteps above their head signaled Nettie's presence just before she called down, "Charlie, we're all set. Take your time down there, though."

"I gotta get back online, anyway," Ethan said, gesturing to the bottle. "You can take that if you want."

"I think I'll let you hang on to it," she said, still sputtering and salivating to get the taste out of her mouth.

"Well come back again and finish it off," he said. She could tell the invitation felt awkward in his mouth.

She swallowed hard and handed the bottle back to him. "Look, man. I never got to talk to you after the funeral, but better late than never. I'm really sorry about Gentry," she said. "Most of us would've done more if we'd known how bad off he was."

Ethan twisted his headphone wire around one finger, then another. "You going to the ceremony next week? They're turning my dad's garage into a fire station, if you haven't heard."

"So they say. Are you going?" She glanced around the basement.

"Fuck that," he said.

She laughed. "If you ask me, a match and some kerosene would do that place some good."

Ethan finally pulled the headset onto his ears and turned away from her. "I couldn't agree more."

On her way back into town, Charlie lingered at the stop sign in front of Earl's Auto Services & Supply, which loomed in a sea of dead Queen Anne's lace and overgrown pampas grass. It was built haphazardly in the 1970s with every material imaginable—brick, metal, glass, plastic, wood, stone, cement—and one of the giant doors was starting to fall off its chains. Weeds grew into old tires in the little green-space off to the left side, and the remnants of black oil puddles stained the broken pavement out front.

The window was broken in Jackson Hatcher's old office at the front of the building. He was Earl's assistant manager, and he was in jail, now. The family's little double-wide was up for sale. Charlie's dad said not even the Mexican immigrants at the textile plant wanted it. Charlie had always wondered what happened in that trailer, and she was sure Dale knew. Bethany was like a nice Persian rug that had been stapled into place over a damp floor for a hundred years. Peel up a corner and see what you find.

She got a text that Tuesday evening from Nettie, who was passing along a message from Ethan, who had no need for a cell phone. He had a new game and was wondering if she wanted to come play. The words "please God come spend time with my agoraphobic son" weren't there, but Charlie heard them all the same. She pulled on her cleanest dirty pair of jeans and a long-sleeved black t-shirt that she hoped made her look thinner than she felt, brushed her dark hair, and fingered through her mother's makeup and dime-store body sprays before giving up and getting in the truck.

Nettie was in the garden. She waved when Charlie honked.

"I'm here," Ethan said when she knocked on the door-frame. She hoped she wasn't imagining a happy lilt in his voice. When she went downstairs, he was sitting on the couch watching a Japanese cartoon with subtitles, drinking fruit punch from a straw. The faded green Zelda shirt he wore matched his eyes.

"I'm going to finish out this episode, but here." He pressed a button on the game controller and handed it to her. "Try this out. It's Grand Theft. Nothing like stealing drugs and shooting cops on a Tuesday night, right?" When he laughed, it was a dry, hollow sound, almost a cough.

"Will I, like, mess anything up?"

"I started you your own file. Mess up all you want."

Her fingers were awkward on the controller. She blew herself up more than once learning the buttons, but she got better once the cartoon was over and Ethan started coaching her. He wasn't too pushy, and taught her to laugh when she got hurt or died. "No pressure. Try again," he kept saying. "Ugh, that happens to me all the time. Try again. This time, go the other way. Oops. Try again. That spot can be a little glitchy. No pressure."

She heard a small clicking sound coming from his direction every few seconds, and when the game was reloading after her fifth death, Charlie looked down at his hands to see him picking at some dry skin on his thumb. The pads of all his fingers were marked and scarred.

"Nervous habit," he said when he caught her staring.

"You nervous?" she asked.

"Always."

"Well, I know you're on that teetotal thing, but. . ."

"I'm down."

They passed the bottle of Maker's back and forth, making faces and shuddering and laughing. She passed the controller to him. "There. Now play until you're not nervous anymore."

When the liquor finally kicked in, he started talking and couldn't stop. He talked about how his old girlfriend Mary Stuart had three kids of three different colors, and how his cousin Gregory crashed his truck off the bridge last year. He told her about the four months he worked at the funeral home in high school, how he didn't have to deal with the bodies but had to clean up the embalming room when they were done, which was almost worse. He told her about the girls who watched his stream, dressed as his favorite video game characters, and sent him unsolicited, faceless photos of their tits. By the time they were to the point of chasing swigs of bourbon with fruit punch, they were engaged in a brief argument over an unfair Pokemon trade in middle school. "I had just started collecting them," she groaned, head swirling. "How was I supposed to know you were ripping me off?"

"Because yours was fucking shiny and the one I wanted to give you wasn't," he said, hiccupping through his laughter. "You always hold on to anything that's shiny. Guard shiny shit with your life. That's like . . . life lesson number one."

She fell backward onto the couch's arm. "Shiny shit," she echoed, mellowing.

"You know, the weirdest thing about what I do now is that I always hated playing video games in front of people. Gentry used to sit behind me while I played, and he was the biggest ass about it. Backseat driver. He might as well have been holding the controller the way he tried to tell me what to do every two seconds and the way he got on my case whenever I screwed up. It made me so anxious that I started not wanting to play in front of him until I got good enough at the game to not need his help, and then I just didn't want to play in front of anyone."

"I guess that's one thing you're not nervous about anymore."

"I guess not," he said, then he looked right at her. "It's weird. Gentry was a lot more tolerant of the fact that I'm gay than he was with the fact that I was shitty at video games."

The swig of bourbon she was taking fell down her windpipe and she choked on it.

"Sorry," he said, like he'd stepped on her toe. "Sorry, sorry."

She sputtered, the heat rising from her lungs to her cheeks. "No, I just swallowed wrong. I'm not. . . " she coughed. "Well, yeah, I mean. That's. Yeah, that's cool. I bet he was surprised. Not that I'm surprised. I mean, I am . . . well, hey, that's cool. I just never would've guessed."

He seemed amused. "My rainbow flags and Madonna posters got lost in the mail. And no, I'm not going to go shopping with you."

"No, I mean," she coughed again. He went to the mini-fridge on the other side of the room. She said, "I'm totally, you know, chill. It doesn't matter to me."

Ethan tossed her a cold bottle of water. "Drink that and chill out."

She did. "So Gentry knew?" she asked.

"He was the only person who did," he said. "He figured it out just a few months after I figured it out, actually, a few years after high school. Men liking men wasn't something I even knew was possible for a long time. It wasn't exactly in the movies or shows I watched or the books I read or the video games I played. But Gentry found the wrong kind of website on my computer one night and took me for a ride in his new truck to get milkshakes. He asked me in the drive-thru of a McDonald's. He was cool about it, actually. Since he was a junkie and I was a faggot, he said we could be outcasts together."

He paused for a moment, then looked at her as though just remembering she was there. "But no one else around here knows. Except you, now."

Charlie couldn't imagine Gentry being cool about something like that, but Dale had known him much better than she did. That must have been not long before he died. "Tell me something," she said.

"Sirius is the brightest star."

"Not that," she said. "Did you really find Gentry's body?"

"Yeah."

"Shit, dude."

He sat back down. "Working at the funeral home before that helped. Dead bodies were kind of objects to me at that point. I'm just glad it wasn't Mom that walked up on him. I think she thinks that was what messed me up," he gestured vaguely to the basement. "But I was already kind of messed up by then." She nodded, remembering how withdrawn he was in middle school and high school. "Hey, is it going to bore you if I play? It helps me relax."

"Go ahead," she said. "I like watching."

Ethan was really quiet for the rest of that night, like he was spent. She hadn't meant to dredge up difficult topics but the alcohol made her more curious than tactful and it obviously made him more open than he was normally. The controller in his hands kept him from picking at his fingers, but once the alcohol started wearing off, his hands started to shake, then his foot. He started making pretty careless mistakes on the game he was playing.

"This is why I don't drink," he said, when the silence became awkward.

"Anything I can do?"

"I think I'm just gonna go to bed," he said, turning off the television. "Sleep it off. Do you want to come over after your shift this weekend? We can spend all night Saturday getting shit-faced so you can go to Dale's ceremony on Sunday hungover."

"I'm not going to that shit. But I can come back over if you're up for it?" she asked, hopefully.

"I am."

That Saturday morning, Charlie pulled her book bag out of the closet and dug out the baggies of anti-anxiety pills she'd stolen from Stephen. She found all of the round yellow tablets, combined them into one bag, and put them in the pocket of her winter coat before heading out for her shift at the farmers market.

Austin's Grill on Main Street looked like a seventies magazine ad: plump booths and chairs that had seen better days, tin signs with old-fashioned Coke ads, and a color-smeared whiteboard with the daily specials scrawled onto it. Once, when Charlie was a kid, she wrenched herself free of her mother's hand, dipped between the legs of the people in line, under the counter, and into the kitchen. The first thing she saw was a cracked floor of mud-red brick tiles splattered with grease, then dripping pipes sinking from a ceiling that had obviously endured more than one minor explosion. A lone mouse ran beneath the refrigerator. Patty, an abrasive, leathery woman who sang in the choir at church, ushered her back out to her mother, who jerked her wrist hard and told her to straighten up. As picture perfect as it was in the front, Charlie never forgot what she'd seen in the back.

When she walked in, Charlie saw the same old men at the table in the front who had been drinking coffee from those same thick green mugs every morning since she was a child. If not for the fact that their wives used to be her troop leaders and Sunday School teachers, she would've wondered if these men had homes at all, or if they were lost boys living full-time at the diner, shaking their newspapers, grumbling at muddy cleats and short shorts, waitresses topping off their coffee from sunrise to sunset.

It was still dark outside when Charlie stepped up to the counter after waiting in line behind a few more Saturday early risers. They patted her shoulder, asked how she'd been since she moved away. Where were you at, again? Is it nice there? How long have you been gone? Have you seen Dale since you been back? Whatever happened with that, anyway? Did you hear about Earl's? Living at your Mama's now?

She called them each by name, if she could remember their name, and if she couldn't, she gave them a cheery but impersonal "Hey, you."

The steam from her breath led her back down Main Street. A speaker's platform was being erected in front of the garage, and silver bleachers had been dragged across the street from the elementary school soccer field for the choir to stand on.

Nettie was arranging collards on the table when Charlie walked up, puffing from the cold. She reached into her pocket immediately and passed over the baggie. Nettie held it awkwardly, staring at the little yellow pills inside.

"Klonopin," Charlie said, pointing. Nettie looked at her without moving, the baggie still in front of her face. "They're mine. Well . . ." Charlie made a face and tilted her head. "Maybe not originally, but they're mine *now*." Nettie raised an eyebrow. "They *weren't* mine, but then they *were*, and now they *are*, so I can do what I want with them and I want y'all to have them." She paused. When Nettie didn't speak, she said, "They're one milligram tablets. I usually cut mine in half and that's enough but if that doesn't work taking a full one is fine—at least that's what I've heard. If he's been on them before he shouldn't see any, like, side effects or anything."

If she weren't so committed to giving Ethan a way to take the edge off of his anxiety, she'd regret this entirely.

"Don't you need them?" Nettie asked, with an incredulous note.

"Yes," Charlie said. "But I can go to the doctor and get a prescription like Dale does. Maybe these will help him get there, too."

"Thank you."

"Don't mention it," Charlie said. "Really. Don't mention it to anyone."

"Mornin', ladies."

"Christ," Nettie barked, throwing the pills into her pocket right as Dale ducked his head into the tent from the side.

"Well hey, you," Charlie blurted out, like an expletive. Her face exploded with heat, and she could hear the crinkle of Nettie shoving the baggie deeper into her pocket. As though choreographed months before, Dale and Charlie both dropped their eyes to the other person's left hand. His was there. Hers wasn't.

"Oh," both of them said at the same time.

Nettie leaned way back in her chair before pushing herself to her feet, and lighting a cigarette. "I'm going to go for a walk."

Dale gestured at the cigarette. "We try to keep the market smoke free."

"Fuck off," Nettie said, not even looking behind her.

"Well," Dale said to Charlie. "How was Rock Hill?"

She tried to detect sarcasm, bitterness, hostility, or even just discomfort in his voice, but it wasn't there, and that pissed her off. "Better than here," she said, coolly.

"Ah, okay." He paused. "That makes sense."

Charlie didn't know what was okay, or what about it made sense to him. He cleared his throat and held his duty belt on both sides, tilting his body back just slightly. He creaked. She stared a little too long at his broad chest and felt her body repulsing in the other direction. *A little too Captain America for me.* "Did you hear about Earl Coats' garage?" he asked after a few more seconds of silence.

"Yes, Dale," she said, instantly furious and wishing she'd saved just one of the anxiety pills for herself. "Everyone has heard about your motherfucking garage. Congratulations."

"I'm sorry. It's just, I'm speaking at the ceremony tomorrow, so I'd like you to be there. It would set a good example, you know, if we're still supportive of one another."

"Did you think I wasn't supportive?" Charlie said.

"Now, where would I get that idea?" he said. Finally, some sarcasm.

"No, Dale. I was always really fucking proud. Do you know that? Protecting and serving and fighting fires and being a knight in shining armor to everyone but me." Her voice turned to slime in her mouth. Their marriage was hanging over her head like a guillotine.

"I don't think that's a healthy way of looking at this."

"I don't give a fuck. You want to *help people*. That's all you want to do is *help people*, right? I'm so lucky to be married to someone who just wants to *help people*."

His forehead rumpled like a basset hound's, mouth set in a weird lopsided scowl. "Don't be like that. Folks worried when you took off. Your mama said she didn't even get an address."

"You know the only person who would ever believe me about you is Nettie," she said. "And that's just because she's looking for excuses to keep hating you."

"Believed you about me?" he asked. "What is it you think I did to you?"

"Throwing shit at my head? Yelling all the time? Keeping me awake for days on end? Starting arguments for no damn reason, just because you wanted a reason to fight someone and I was the only person you had available?"

"I was sick, Charlie. I couldn't help what I did. But I am sorry. In therapy they tell you to take responsibility, even if you felt like you had no control at the time. I would've explained, but you were gone when I got out of the hospital. Then I wanted to send you papers but we had no idea where you were."

"Bring them by the house."

"I'd rather we meet for dinner and talk before making any big decisions. I've been wanting to talk to you anyway, about other things."

"If you've got papers, I'll sign them."

"It'd be better for you around here if people at least see you try. I need for you to try."

"If you've got papers, I'll sign them."

"I have a mental illness, Charlotte. I'm getting treatment now. I couldn't help it."

"Bring your papers by the house, Dale."

"I didn't know if you were ever coming home."

"Good morning, sir," she said. "Do you want to buy some collards?"

"Christ." He creaked his way out of the tent.

Nettie came back into the tent about thirty seconds later. "Welp," she said, and fell back into her lawn chair. It didn't sound like she'd walked in from very far away, like maybe she'd been listening just on the other side of the tent.

Charlie had not moved. She was still standing, leaning forward slightly, shoulders shrugged and squared to the empty space where her husband had been. Her whole body was hot, except for her toes. Those were numb.

"I know this isn't a very Jesus thing of me to say," Nettie said. "But I really do hate that kid." She slapped the register until the door shot open. Then she started flicking through the dollar bills inside. "Sick or not."

"He didn't do anything wrong," Charlie said. "He's never done anything wrong. That's his problem. If anyone has a problem with him, it's always the other person's fault, because he's never done anything wrong."

Nettie was quiet for a few minutes as she flicked the money with her thumb from one hand to another. That gave Charlie the time she needed to feel bad about what she'd said. She was definitely being harder on him than she should've been, perhaps.

"I *am* glad he finally went and got help," Charlie said, almost to herself. "Treatment, you know. Medicine. All of that stuff. He seems to be doing okay. Even when I left, just knowing he was at the hospital where he couldn't hurt himself made me feel better."

"Well, if anyone needs help now, I reckon it's him," she said. "I don't like him but I don't wish walking up on a dead kid on anyone."

Charlie looked at her.

"Oh, yeah. It'll be . . . three weeks ago, now?" Nettie said. "He was the one that found Hatcher's little girl. Brains blown out all over the ground. Eight years old."

Charlie's legs gave out and she fell into a chair and looked at Nettie, who went on to explain that Dale had smelled something funny over there after Jackson's wife, Sarah, a friend of Dale's family, ended up in the hospital from a mysterious *car accident* that absolutely no one in town had actually witnessed. So Dale went to check up on the rest of them of them one morning. The oldest daughter (neither she nor Charlie could remember her name or face for how hidden Jackson kept her) was already gone by the time he got there. Jackson started hollering and ordering Dale off the property, and by the time he got back with a warrant, Sarah was dead in the hospital, and the youngest girl had run off, too.

Dale spent two straight days looking for the girls in the woods before he walked right up on the little girl laying in the leaves with a bullet through her head and the gun on the ground. They found enough evidence of sexual abuse on her that they were able to get Jackson behind bars. The oldest was still missing, long gone without a trace, and probably dead as well.

People in the town weren't talking about it the way they should've been, Nettie said. Just like drug addiction, they didn't want to believe that things like this happened in *their town*, so they pretended it didn't happen at all. "Pisses me off," Nettie said. "Like if they close their eyes, it won't exist. Who knows how many other kids around here are going through it? They act like this was isolated. Maybe it was. But Jesus Christ, what if it's not?"

Charlie's hands were shaking violently. She fumbled in her jacket pocket for a cigarette and held the first drag in her lungs for a few seconds longer than she would have normally. Dale graduated from basic law enforcement training thinking he'd catch some people speeding and maybe navigate a few house robberies before retiring, if he was lucky. He wanted to be the town hero for the rest of his life, and he was still on track to do that on the outside. But she knew him well enough to know that something inside him had to have flipped after this.

For the first time in a while, she didn't think about Dale the way he was right before he was hospitalized—raising hell every night, scaring her to death. She thought about how much he wanted to help everyone, and how she was included in that category no matter how much she wanted to be set apart and separate and special in his eyes. She didn't want to be down on the town's level, gazing up at him in all of his goodness. She thought about how quickly she grew to resent that feeling.

Her eyes scanned the market, but Dale was gone. Charlie wasn't sure what she would do if he weren't. He'd never needed her help before, but she always seemed to need his. She had needed his shoulder, his arms, his chest to cry into. She'd needed to trust his voice telling her that everything would be fine. She needed him like the whole town needed him, and for the same reason . . . an anchor, a rock. Security. But soon she realized that he would never need her in that way. He would always be the superhero and she would always, always, *always* be a helpless groupie.

It was bizarre and uncomfortable to think about him needing help. *Her* help, for once.

"I wish I had known," she said still scanning the crowd. "When he was here talking to me. I'd have, I don't know."

"Well," Nettie said, moaning a little as she stood up like her body weighed a ton. "I'm heading home. I hear I'm getting too old to be out here this long every day. Wrap up here and bring the truck by my place. We'll be there."

Charlie knew why Nettie wanted her to do that and she didn't care.

She closed thirty minutes early and backed the truck right up into the grass by the tent, tossing bunches of collards into the bed as fast as she could. She bypassed her mother in the kitchen and jumped directly into the shower, toes burning as she leaned against the wall, facing the faucet, supporting herself with both hands on the wall. *No pressure, no pressure, no pressure.*

Nettie was waiting on the porch when Charlie pulled up at the farm and started unloading. "I got it," the old woman said, coming down the stairs and jerking a thumb at the door. "I told him you were coming. Told him you had a . . . weird day."

Charlie went inside and knocked on the doorpost leading down into the basement. The door was open. "I'm here," Ethan said, just as he had the day before, as if her knocking were a question. He had a bottle waiting for her when she hit the last stair.

"I saw Dale today," she said.

"Mom told me."

She turned the bottle up and held her nose so she could take three giant swallows. "He wants to sign papers, or talk about why we shouldn't or something."

"That's petty. All you did was run off on him when he got sick with a mental illness to go work for a drug dealer."

"Shut up."

When the whiskey hit her, and it didn't take long, Charlie tried not to fight the drunk swirl of the room. She tried to go with it, to let it sweep her farther and farther around until the twist became too much and her chest tightened up to make it stop. She wanted to talk. She wanted him to ask her questions, so she could dig back down into herself for the answers and maybe arrive somewhere she hadn't been yet, some corner of her mind that was still able to think clearly. Charlie imagined all of her hard secrets and fears and sins rising to the surface, slow and thick, like air bubbles in a jar of honey turned upside down.

Instead, Ethan sat silently. She wasn't looking directly at him but she could feel him watching her. Then, he got up, and suddenly went digging in a few boxes by his bed. "Hey, you wanna give me a hand with something?"

"I really don't think a video game is in the cards for me right now, man."

"No, let's go get some food. I'm hungry."

"Yeah, okay. Wait?" She sat up and looked at him.

"Just a honey bun from the gas station or something."

"You want to go to the gas station?"

"I want to go," he said.

Charlie didn't know what her response should be. She gauged his face and saw nothing but a strange calmness. He dug a coat out of a box and stumbled against his desk chair trying to put it on. She'd only just realized that he'd been drinking, too.

"Don't you have something to eat here?" she asked, nervously. "We can get breakfast from Austin's tomorrow if you want. I don't think we need to be driving."

"No, I've wanted to get rid of these for a while." He knelt down and hoisted the cardboard box of liquor into his arms. The glass bottles sang against each other like bells. "And I know how I want to do it."

"All right," she said. It was as good a reason to die in a ditch as any, and if Dale found them, maybe she could hang on to life just long enough to say she was sorry. Maybe the town would forgive her, if she used her last breath asking for it.

The stairs tilted right on their way up; both of them leaned hard against the left wall, letting it guide them forward. Ethan didn't hesitate at the threshold of the basement and kitchen, stepping out onto the porch like he'd done it every single day for the last three years. The only indicator he gave that he was shocked by the sensation of the outdoors was the jolt of the cold air in his shoulders. He stopped and stood for a moment at the top of the porch stairs. She leaned against the rail beside him.

"I *just* got you some meds," she said with a small laugh.

"Yeah? I probably still need them."

Then he went down the stairs, marched down the sidewalk and threw open the door to a two-car shed across the driveway. Gentry's truck was there. Ethan lifted the box over the tailgate, and laid it carefully into the bed. Nettie must have been keeping it clean and functioning, because when he jerked the key off the wall and started it, it purred to life.

"Do you even still have a license?"

"I don't plan on getting pulled over," he said. "Get in."

Charlie climbed in, leaned back, and started testing different parts of her face with her fingers. Her lips always went numb first when she was drunk. The truck smelled like cigarettes. "Go five over. Dale always says you can always tell a drunk because they're hauling ass, dragging ass, or kissing ass. Five over."

He put the truck into gear and turned the talk radio station to a comfortable level. An oil rig had exploded in Finland, killing dozens of workers, and it was important to consider the worldwide consequences of the disaster. Charlie could not have possibly felt farther away from Finland in that moment. Another planet was dealing with that problem. Another species. The old men at the front table of Austin's would work out the implications of it tomorrow morning over coffee so she wouldn't have to.

Ethan took the corners smooth, but his foot jumped on the brake at stop signs, like he was testing how much pressure it really took to stop something that big in its tracks.

"Where are we going?" Charlie asked when they passed the gas station with the flickering lottery light.

"You said you'd help me get rid of these."

"I said I could go for a honey bun," she said, expecting to see Dale's cruiser around every corner or sitting at every intersection.

When the truck finally stopped, Charlie slid out onto concrete and leaned hard on the door to close it again. When she focused her eyes, Ethan was climbing out of the truck with a determined and hostile look on his face. He dropped the tailgate and pulled the box of liquor into his arms.

"Come on," he said, offering his elbow. "Lean on me."

She held his sleeve and let him guide her under an ailing

garage door and inside what was left of Earl's Auto Services & Supply, the soon-to-be Bethany Fire Station #2.

Ethan dropped the box and pulled out a bottle of green-label Jack. His expression contorted when he took a swallow.

"Dad drinks green-label Jack," she noted absently. "Said it was a man's drink."

"My dad was never much of a man at all," Ethan said, distantly.

"You're one to talk," Charlie muttered. "Agoraphobic my foot."

"Gentry either, but at least he never became a father." He said the word like it was a curse, then threw the bottle of liquor against an overturned shelving unit. It shattered, and the sound made her jump and throw up her hands, expecting flying spaghetti. Charlie had never sobered up so quickly.

"Jesus Christ!" she hissed. Ethan shoved a bottle into her hand and wrapped his fingers around hers until he was sure she was holding it.

"You're fucking insane," she pleaded. "You're fucking insane, dude. The ceremony is tomorrow."

"Throw it," he said.

"No." She tried to hand it back to him.

"Do it."

"I'm not drunk anymore."

"Even better," he said, staring at her with intense green eyes. "Throw it."

She looked around. "Where?"

"Wherever you want." He took a step back. "We're not decorating."

Charlie looked at the bottle. It was Woodford Reserve, barely touched. The glass was thick and heavy. Her finger smeared at the dust to see the trees on the label and, in doing so, she dropped it at her feet. She yelped and jumped as the glass shattered and splashed her legs with bourbon.

"That's okay," he said, throwing a bottle of orange vodka against a far wall. "Try again."

"Is this all of it?" Charlie asked.

"It's all his." He handed her another bottle. She took it, but hesitated. He reared his arm back and lifted his leg like a baseball player, and the bottle splattered against a window frame and exploded into wet shards. His first time out of the house in years, and this was how he wanted to spend it, and somehow he'd decided that she was the person worth spending it with.

She threw her bottle gracelessly, but braver. Thinking of Dale helped. He'd get here tomorrow morning and see his precious project all soaked in alcohol and shimmering from broken glass and broken windows and they'd all talk about crazy kids and delinquents. Looking at Ethan, at the furious way he rattled through the bottles, she could see that was exactly what they were: two Bethany children determined to have the last laugh, only none of it was funny.

Ethan handed her another bottle, and she chucked it quickly against the plexiglass office wall. "We're not doing anything wrong," he said.

"Is that what we're going to tell the cops when they show up?" she asked.

"I don't owe anyone in this town an explanation. Do you?"

She felt like a bug, suspended in amber, perfectly preserved. No matter what she decided to do or where she decided to go, this place—with him—was the safest place she was ever going to be.

Charlie wondered which of his three uniforms Dale was

planning on wearing to the ceremony, whether he planned to dress as a United States Air Force veteran, a volunteer firefighter, or a police officer. She knew how to wash each of those uniforms by hand. She had ironed all of them herself, fingered the hems of the pants so she could hang them in the closet just so, stitched the insignia across his chest right down to the millimeter, but in their nearly two years of marriage, she had never wondered—as she wondered now—what it felt like for him to have that many choices, that many varieties of goodness just waiting in his closet. Was it a gift? Was it a burden? Was it lonely up there on a hill too steep for her to climb?

"Do you ever miss Gentry?" she asked.

Ethan had his arms folded, panting, taking a break. "He was an ass."

"Is that why you've been hiding in the basement since he died?"

Ethan looked at her. "You think I'm hiding?"

"Aren't you?"

Ethan fished into his pocket for a moment. "You know what he really told me when he figured it out?"

"What?"

"That the world would be just as shitty to me as it had been to him, because to people in this town, being a faggot is an illness with no good cure, same as addiction. That's what he thought. That's what they think. He said they'll tell me I need Jesus then they'll tell me I can't go to church. He said they'll try to come up with all these reasons why I am the way I am and how I can fix it. He said we needed to look after one another because no one else was going to look after us. He told me that we could be outcasts together and then he fucking died."

Charlie closed her eyes.

"And for what it's worth," he added, "I don't blame you for not wanting to go home to a man like Dale if you don't feel right doing it. But I can blame you for not taking care of someone you love who has problems like that."

Her eyes stung and a tear fell in the crack between her cheek and nose.

There were two bottles left. He twisted off the caps, and handed one of them to her.

"What should we toast to?" she asked. Her voice was weak.

"To Gentry," he said. "And this goddamn fucking town."

Both of them took a swig and tossed the bottles to the side. Immediately he put a hand inside of his pocket and pulled out a lighter.

It took a second for her to realize what it was. Then she swatted at it, trying to knock it out of his hand.

"You lunatic," she said. "No. No, no, no."

It took four quick cracks for him to bring the lighter to a flame.

"Ethan," she said. She grabbed at his arm. His face glowed orange, intense.

"Charlie," he said. "I'd go outside if I were you. I'll be there in a minute."

"You'll go to jail so fast it'll make your fucking head spin."

"Yeah," he said, laughing a little bit. "I will."

He held the flame away from his chest. His eyes were determined but strangely placid, like he was just ticking off the boxes on a to-do list he'd written long ago, performing a scene he'd practiced in his head for years.

"*I'll* go to jail," she cried. He looked at her. Her heart was trying to come out of her throat along with the whiskey. Her teeth were rattling from nervousness. "Don't you see me standing here with you? I threw some of those bottles. This is already vandalism. Don't make it arson, too."

Ethan stared at her with his eyes watering. Charlie could see that she was a wrench in his plan that he hadn't expected. This was something he was supposed to do alone, and she had gotten in the way.

"You, me, and your mama will pay for this more than your father, or Dale, or Gentry, or anyone else in Bethany," she said. "They don't give a shit. Not really. And they never did. But I do."

He closed his eyes, releasing one thick tear, and she nodded. He clicked the lighter closed and she reached out slowly to take it. He shook his head. "No, it was Gentry's."

"Keep it, then," she said. "Keep it and let's get out of here."

He seemed frozen to the spot, so she tugged at his jacket sleeve to activate him. Then they helped one another through puddles of alcohol and over rusted car parts and broken glass toward the front door. Charlie looked over her shoulder at Nettie's building, at the past that Bethany had stolen from their family—by ostracizing Gentry, neglecting Nettie, then gossiping about Ethan until he didn't even know what person he should be to best satisfy the people of a town he hated.

Their truck doors slammed in sync with one another. The old pick-up groaned to life. Ethan leaned back against his seat and exhaled, then rested his forehead on the wheel.

"I need to get out of here."

Charlie nodded, staring at the dark building looming in front of them. "Yeah, you do."

"This didn't go how I wanted it to go."

"Sorry about that," she said.

"No, it's just . . . it means I've got a lot of explaining to do."

Charlie wondered if he was looking for the reset button, just like she was. Turn the game system on again, off again, on again. *I'll do it right next time. Give me another chance. Please, give me another chance.* Running away was so much easier than trying to figure something out, but figuring it out, for her, could definitely lead to something better.

"You don't owe anyone in this town an explanation. I'll stay." The words felt thick in her mouth as she formed them. "I'll stay and smooth things over."

He lifted his face from the steering wheel and looked at her. "Are you sure?"

"I'll talk to Dale. I'll make it work." Then, quieter, "I'll make all of it work."

"*All* of it?"

Charlie hesitated, looking out the window and exhaling. Her chest seemed a lot emptier than it was earlier in the night, like she'd been wrung out, like after all this time there was finally space for something better to get in there and grow. "It's worth a try. But if nothing else I'll talk to him and make sure you don't catch heat. "

"I owe you one."

"You get out of here, and don't come back until you're ready. That's more than enough."

On the way back to the farm, Ethan's knuckles were white on the wheel, and the eerie blue light of Gentry's stereo system reflected in his eyes. He had picked the lock on his own mind and let himself out. He was gone. She had picked the lock on her life and let herself back in. She was home. Ethan reached over the console to take her wrist. He brought the heel of her palm to his mouth and rested it there, watching the road over her fingers for a moment before letting go. She touched his shoulder and let her hand fall back to her leg. There was nothing but dark in front of them, and the faint orange glow of Bethany streetlights in the rearview mirror.

GREEN PASTURES

A WOMAN LIVING IN HIS BARN was the last thing Ethan needed. He'd seen her sneaking in and out over the last week, but tried to blow it off, hoping it was just some kid on a dare. But last Monday, when the sun was just right, he could see that it was definitely a woman, and she definitely knew she was trespassing. Ethan made eye contact with her as he was waiting for the laundry to finish up in the machine on the back porch. She froze like a scared rabbit, then quickly wedged the heavy door open far enough to slip inside and disappear. It didn't seem worth a call to the police, and he didn't know the phone number for the cops out here anyway.

Ethan couldn't help but wonder about the mind of a person willing to live in a barn. He spent the last few days sitting in the living room with his feet on his desk, playing video games and glancing out the window every few minutes. Maybe she was a killer, and his barn was full of decomposing bodies. Or maybe she was a bank robber and needed a place to hide the cash.

On his way into town for groceries the next day, Ethan drove the dirt trail along the property looking for a car or truck parked in some inconspicuous place in case someone had come to spy on him (his latest theory), but he didn't find one. So maybe she really was just hiding.

Ethan had left the town of Bethany six months ago, fleeing to the first safe spot he could find, far enough away to feel like he was in a different place, but not so far that it made him feel isolated and nervous. He lived for a week in a hotel before finding this house for rent. The old tobacco barn was listed as an *exclusive feature* on the website. Ethan assumed it was infested with all kinds of unsavory wildlife and thus had no desire to set foot inside it. From the doorway, it smelled like a box of wet cigarettes, and the outside lean-to had collapsed into a pile of wood beams and tin. There was certainly nothing in there to steal, unless she was digging for tobacco-curing antiques. But she wasn't taking anything in or out.

Ethan came home one afternoon to find a ratty blue tarp hanging over the door of the barn to help keep out the dew. She'd laid a few pieces of broken sheet metal from inside the barn over the windows, making it impossible for anyone to see in or out. All pretenses gone, just like that.

His house was smaller than most garages, miles from the towns on either side. It sat on the northern side of a humped Carolina mountain like a gray shoebox on a giant shelf—just a kitchen/living room, bathroom, bedroom, and a closet too tiny to hold anything more than a few shirts and a hefty bag. The only thing Ethan had to steal was his computer, and he was starting to wonder if he'd be better off without it, even if playing video games for money was his only source of income (and his only social life) at the moment. But if she was going to stay for a while—and the practical redecorating loosely indicated that intention—he needed to trust her. This was the most exciting thing that had happened to him since he left town, and as much as he liked his distance from people, he knew from experience that a runaway was not a person, but a living, breathing, walking, talking suitcase full of broken emotional relics that no one could understand even if they pulled them out and brushed the dust off. "Why don't you throw that away?" someone would ask. "That's nothing but junk."

A young guy named Kyle worked the register of the general store down the hill. Ethan became fascinated with him—the relaxed droop of his shoulders, his laugh, the way he could make conversation with anyone who walked in, the casual and almost friendly way that he cursed *to* people and not *at* them. After a few years residing in his mother's basement, Ethan still wasn't comfortable having conversations with strangers, so he kept it short—"Hi, good, hope you are, thanks, have a good one"—and kept his eyes down on the counter.

Ethan walked in one Monday for lunch. The big cowbell knocked against the door with a noise that made him jump. Kyle looked up from a magazine and said, "Hey, man! Feels like I just saw you the other day."

Ethan's heart stopped, then took off running. He looked into Kyle's eyes and felt his tongue thick with disuse. He tried to choose his words as carefully as his mother crafted her Thomas Kincaid puzzles: "Forgot milk."

Kyle nodded. "Yeah. My mom always has a list but I can't really be bothered."

Ethan tried to tilt one side of his mouth up and then lowered his head again, disappearing into the far aisle.

"Well, let me know if I can help you with anything," Kyle called out. Ethan didn't answer.

The woman was on her knees in the yard by the barn when he got home. She was tearing at the ground with her hands and throwing clumps of long grass over her shoulders—first the right, then the left. Ethan descended the hill slowly and quietly, not wanting to startle her. It was only then he noticed five or six brown chickens bobbing around on the other side of the yard, cooing and grumbling at one another.

One of them was lying on the ground. He didn't know much about chicken husbandry—his mother had taken care of the animals after his father left—but Ethan knew enough to know that it was dead.

He walked up behind the woman, and he could see that she was wearing a man's wife beater that looked as though it had been dug out of a donation dumpster. A shiny yellow raincoat was hanging from a rusty nail sticking out of the awning over the lean-to.

"Well, hi there," he finally said.

She jumped up to her feet and whipped around to face him, hands out like she was expecting a few punches. She couldn't have been more than sixteen, gaunt and scared and dirty. It was like walking up on a sick possum, and Ethan immediately showed his hands to indicate he didn't mean any harm.

So the two of them just stood there, facing each other, gaping with their hands up.

Eventually, she pointed her finger at the chickens as though accusing them of something. "I got them from a man down the road," she said, rushed. "He had a sign in front of his house saying they were free."

"I can tell." Ethan jerked a thumb at the dead one.

She looked over his shoulder and then her arms slumped down, disappointed. "The man said not to sneeze in their direction, or they'd fall over and die." The matted brown hair on top of her head stuck straight out of a blue bandana like the stiff branches of a bush, and she had a pale, chiseled white face with sunken eyes and sharp cheekbones. Her eyes in the sun were the dark blue of his father's old Air Force jacket. She was pretty in her own way, like a cliff face in a canyon. Had he been six or seven years younger, and straight . . . well, he probably *still* wouldn't have made a pass at her, but she was nice looking just the same.

"I'm not sure they're supposed to be out in the heat," he said.

"I'm gonna need a jar of river water so the rest don't get sick," she said.

"Pardon?"

"I read it in a book on the bus," she answered. "It's a running water thing. The Indians say running water has healing powers."

"Well, there's a lake about twenty minutes away," Ethan shared. "Or I've got, you know, a faucet in the kitchen."

She twisted the fingers of her hands together anxiously, obviously not a fan of the idea of going up to the house. "Well, I don't really *need* the water."

"What do you got chickens for, anyway?" he asked.

"So I don't have to get eggs from the store," she said, like it should be obvious.

"You can't cook them without a stove."

"Do you have to cook eggs?"

"Yes."

"I can sell them."

"Stores around here don't buy local."

"*Well I didn't know that.*" She sounded offended and eager to end the conversation, but he needed a nice way of asking the only question he really needed an answer to.

"So, how do you like the old place?" he asked.

"I wanna grow a garden." She turned and gestured with a dirty hand toward the patch of grass she was ripping up.

"I don't know the first thing about growing shit. My mom is a farmer in Bethany. She's really good at it, but I never picked it up," Ethan admitted. "Plus, I don't have any tools."

"You're from Bethany?" she asked.

"Yeah." They stood awkwardly for a few more seconds. "I've got some chicken legs in the house."

"Abigail," she blurted.

"Ethan Coats. Abigail who?"

"Just Abigail." She paused for a second. "I like chicken."

She insisted on eating dinner in the yard alone, cross-legged, with the plate in her lap. It was just as well, because he didn't have a kitchen table. Ethan didn't ask her how long it had been since she'd eaten anything substantial. It felt rude to imply that she was homeless, even if it was obvious, and he didn't want to hear any sob stories. He hoped she would afford him the same privacy. His story wasn't one he wanted to tell anyone.

The next day, Ethan drove to the Wal-Mart in the next county to buy a lamp, some blankets, a fan, and several extension cords. He presented them to her, still in the bags. She stood in the doorway of the barn like he was giving her his firstborn instead of some cheap things to make her more comfortable.

"Don't have any way to pay you back," she said.

"I didn't ask you to," he said. "I've got a bunch of old clothes up at the house that don't fit me anymore, if you want them. There's a washer and dryer on the porch and the bathroom is inside. The house is unlocked."

"I can't pay you," she said.

"Did you hear what I said?"

"Yes sir."

"Oh God, don't call me sir."

"Okay."

Then Ethan left her alone. He needed to focus on the new Fallout anyway. It landed him a viewer count of about two-thousand on an average night, and a haul of about fifty dollars in donations per session. Some people liked to play. Some liked to watch. He liked to play, and profited off of those who liked to watch. It wasn't a bad living, but it was oddly isolating to be on camera, on stage in front of an invisible crowd. He had a microphone and had to keep it on to talk for the people asking questions in the chat log. They loved when he called them out by name—or username—to have *their* comment acknowledged out of the hundreds asking, and they were usually the people who donated. So he tried to talk to as many as he could. When the girls flirted with him, he acknowledged it with nervous laughter. When the boys flirted with him, he ignored it, because he had to. And when a night's session was over, he gave his usual sign-off, turned off the stream and the camera and the microphone, and collapsed backward in his chair, as exhausted as any factory worker or doctor or office executive would be after a day's work.

The day after he and Abigail were properly introduced, Ethan went into his closet and dug out his brother Gentry's old gaming system that he'd gotten for Christmas when they were kids. Gamers today would call it *ancient*. Ethan couldn't even use the flat-screen to play it, because it didn't have the right hookups.

He'd bought an old box television from a yard sale down the road when he first moved here just in case he wanted to play one day. When Ethan was seven years old, he had to both win a wrestling match and cry to his mother just to be able to play it. Now that Gentry wasn't there to stand in his way, starting the game felt wrong. Every time his little eight-bit character fell down a hole or off the screen, he wished Gentry would show up and snatch the controller out of his hands. "Let go," he'd say. "You always fuck it up. Let me do it. I don't have all day."

The game didn't have the same magic it had when he was a boy. He left the television and the console out on the floor by the desk, in case he wanted to play it again, though he doubted he would.

Ethan missed his mother, though he'd never (and didn't have to) admit it to her. The night he left, she gave him two hundred dollars in twenties and a pre-paid Wal-Mart cellphone and told him to call—and he did. Before he got in the truck to leave her for the first time in his life, he wrapped his arms around her and told her he was gay.

He would always remember the lift in her shoulders, the deep soul-releasing sigh that indicated a lot of pieces being put together, hopefully about how being gay in a small Southern town and being the one who found his brother's dead body and not being able to say goodbye to his father before he skipped town was enough to drive anyone to live in a basement for three years before fleeing entirely.

Finally she said, "Well son, *I'm* not trying to date you, so I don't really give a shit." And just like that, he'd told his secret to three people—Gentry, Charlie, and his mother. None of them cared. Was that a good thing or a bad thing? He didn't know.

She'd be happier here, he knew, than she was in Bethany, surrounded by people who still looked at her with patronizing sympathy even after all these years. But Gentry's grave was there, and she'd never leave it. He didn't blame her.

He called her one night about a month after Abigail arrived. He hadn't given a lot of thought to how he was going to explain the presence of a teenage girl living on his property. He hoped it would just come up in a way that felt natural. She gave him all the news from Bethany. Pamela Wright, who was older than God and who'd had one foot in the grave for about twenty years since her thyroid cancer diagnosis, finally died. None of the lawyers in town wanted to represent Jackson Hatcher during his trial because of whatever it was he did to those poor kids—one still missing, one dead—so why not just throw him in the electric chair ("Or whatever it is they do these days") and be done with it? Equally scandalous, according to the choir, was that Mary Overton took three Sundays off to get plastic surgery and good for her, no reason why anyone shouldn't look the way they wanna look, life's too damn short. She got it on her eyelids, or eyebrows, or something like that.

Ethan found new lines under his eyes every day. His mother told him that loneliness aged a man quicker than anything. He wasn't bad looking, and had to keep up his physical appearance to a degree for all the hours he spent on the webcam, but the jaw line and cheekbones he had shared with his brother and father were disappearing, sure enough.

"If I had the money I'd get my tits done," she said.

"Mom."

"You like men, don't mean you can't recognize a nice pair of tits." He heard the crinkling of some kind of food container as she settled into her armchair for the night, groaning from farmer's arthritis.

"How's Charlie?" he asked, holding the cellphone between his shoulder and ear so he could keep playing his game.

"Got a real job now at the pharmacy," his mother said over a mouthful of whatever it was she was eating. Charlie had dabbled briefly in selling pills, so the job suited her. "But she's still working with me on the weekends at the farmer's market. Dropped a whole damn container of eggs in the parking lot the other day and my chickens ain't laying much right now."

"Our chickens all died," he said, not paying attention.

"Since when do you keep chickens?" she asked.

Ethan paused the game and looked out of the front window at Abigail, who was sitting on the railing of the porch, kicking her legs and bumping the pickets softly with her feet. She was slowly getting more comfortable with being near the house, even if being close to him still made her act anxious and weird.

"My tenant kept them." *Tenant* was the word he decided upon in a hurry.

"The hell'd you get a tenant?" his mother asked.

"She just kind of . . . showed up."

"From where?"

"I don't know."

"She older than you?"

Abigail kicked one foot a little too hard and wobbled before grabbing the post to steady herself.

"Not exactly."

"Younger?"

"Yep."

"How much younger?"

"A bit younger."

"Then she had to of come from somewhere."

"Well she's not very divulging," he said, firmly. "And if she wants to keep her silence, she can keep her silence. I'm keeping mine, Lord knows."

When they wrapped up, Ethan went out onto the back porch to take a break from the game and let his eyes rest on the darkness. Abigail was moving laundry from the washer, and when she started the dryer, she lifted herself on top of it and said, "Charlie is a girl's name?"

It took him a minute to realize that she had heard at least part of the conversation. He hoped he hadn't said anything to offend her. "Her real name is Charlotte, but everyone in Bethany calls her Charlie. She's an old friend."

"I like that," Abigail said distantly. "An 'old friend.' Like a friend you've had for a long time, or a friend you had once but don't have anymore, or a friend that's just old. Is your mama mad that I'm here?"

"Nah. It's not the strangest thing she's ever heard of."

"But I'm sixteen and you're . . . older, you know?"

"Yeah, that'd be weird to most folks. But she knows I'm not interested in you." He couldn't resist looking at her face to see if she'd catch his meaning.

"Why?"

Obviously not.

"I'm just not," he said. "And like you said, I'm too old for you anyway."

"I'm used to that."

His stomach dropped. "Do older men usually like you?"

"Me and my little sister. Older men liked us. Or an older

man I guess. Just one." She seemed at peace with the information, or numb about it, staring out into the dark like they were discussing the weather.

"I didn't know you had a little sister," he said.

"I do," she said, emphasizing the present tense. "But that was why I left where I was before. Got tired of that man liking me."

Ethan studied her closely for perhaps the first time since she'd shown up on his property. He looked at her steady eyes, her stringy hair, her hands as they pulled tiny threads from the hem of her shirt. She definitely didn't look like a victim, but he also had no clue what victims looked like, if they looked like anything at all.

"Well, *I* don't like you," he said, firmly. "And my dad was a jackass, too." It was a horribly risky, disgusting guess that he desperately hoped she would correct.

"The stars are out," she said dreamily. "That's Orion. His left shoulder is Betelgeuse. I read it in a book."

"On the bus?" he said.

"Yeah. On the bus."

After a while Ethan figured out that it wasn't attraction that drove him to the store three times a week. It was jealousy. He was jealous. He wanted to be like Kyle, in the same way that he wanted to be like Gentry when they were kids.

The store was a twenty minute drive away, only because he had to circle back around Tusquittee Bald to get to that intersection, but it was a nice ride. He tried to go at different times of the day so he could see the sun rising or setting or sitting over the mountain or hiding behind rain clouds. He wanted to stop and take photos of the scene for his mother, but he knew his phone was too crappy to capture anything other than the landscape and not what he felt when he looked at it.

This time, Kyle was down on the floor in front of the tall glass coolers, arranging Gatorades on the bottom shelf. Ethan decided he wanted a Gatorade, so he took two laps down the toilet paper aisle first and then walked to the coolers. Kyle was reaching into the back, his head buried, which left Ethan with a predicament. Clear his throat? Drop something? Yodel?

He muttered, "S'cuse me" and then reached. He moved his hand past Kyle's ear just far enough for him to notice it was there, and when he did, he jumped. He had earbuds in, listening to something pop-y.

"Hoo, *man*. You, like, scared me to death. Sorry about that. What can I get you?"

"Orange."

"Orange soda?"

"Gatorade."

Kyle reached in and grabbed a bottle, then hopped onto his feet and stood up. "I'll getcha up here," he said, pointing at the register.

The store had a proper western-style interior—candy and soap in barrels, etc.—which Ethan liked it. The décor reminded him of Austin's Grill back in Bethany, the scent of dark wood, antiques, and old-school metal signs that you'd find in an ice cream parlor from the fifties.

"You're in here a lot. Live close by?"

"Past sixty-four."

Kyle nodded. "Good country out there."

Ethan had never been sure what that phrase meant. He passed his debit card over the counter, and Kyle swiped it.

"You need a bag?"

"No."

"All right. Take care Ethan," Kyle said, handing him the bottle, which Ethan almost dropped in shock.

On the way home, Ethan kept the radio off and massaged the steering wheel until his knuckles were white and his veins were bulging. His upper lip was sweating a little bit by the time he arrived at the house. Abigail was on the porch folding laundry when he got out of the truck. He wasn't angry, but he slammed the door loud enough to make her yelp.

"Sorry," he said. "I'm scaring a lot of people today."

"It's okay," she relaxed a little. "You okay?"

"Just . . . just . . ." Oh, hell. "I'm trying to figure out why someone knows my name."

Abigail flicked a pair of pants. "You don't want people to know your name?"

"Well no, I don't really care, it's just, if someone knows my name and they're not supposed to, then I get a little . . . you know?"

She pursed her lips and grabbed a shirt out of the dryer. "Who knew that wasn't supposed to?"

"This guy at the store I go to a lot."

She made a *mmm* sound that indicated she was either thinking hard or being dismissive. He didn't know her well enough, yet, to tell which.

Ethan sat down on the low porch step and put his elbows behind him, leaning back. He had a few minutes before his live stream was scheduled to start; after that, he'd be stuck in front of the screen for the rest of the night.

It got even hotter as the summer wore on. The fog hung heavier every morning and stuck around longer. His black truck was coated with pollen he wouldn't bother to hose off until October. Warm weather was always hard for him, for some reason. He liked the winter—he liked hibernating—and when the weather got hot he felt more pressure to be outside and visible in ways he didn't want to be.

Abigail finished up the laundry a few minutes later and then slammed the door of the old dryer, snapping him out of his thoughts. She scooped the small pile of his old clothes in her arms and walked down the steps, past him.

"Ain't your name on your card thingy?" she asked.

When he didn't answer, she gave him a small, nervous smile, and turned around to shuffle through the grass, barefoot, down to the barn.

Over the next few weeks, Abigail moved from sitting on the porch to leaning by the door, then from the door to the entryway, the entryway to the bathroom, and finally the kitchen, sweeping or shyly tapping spoons on the counter along with whatever music was playing on his computer. She seemed intrigued by the chill-step and trance tracks he played in the background of his streaming sessions—little-known basement DJs from Australia, Tokyo, and Greece.

Sometimes he'd bring things home to her from the store and she ate them on the floor of the kitchen where she watched him live stream every night. The first time he jokingly turned the camera at her—"Say hi to my little sister, everyone!"—she shrieked and hid her face. The second time he did it, she gave a little wave. "How many people are watching?" she asked.

"Four hundred and seventy-six," he answered. Her face went pale and he laughed.

An ugly old hound wandered down off of Jack-Top one muggy morning. They had been sitting on the porch of the house eating cereal when he came up, tail so far between his legs that it was hard to tell a gender. Abigail got an Oatmeal Creme Pie and threw it into the grass and he pushed it around for a few seconds. Hungry dogs are hungry. Starving dogs are suspicious.

"Well he's yours, now," Ethan told her when he finally devoured the pie. "He'll never leave."

She named him Tucup, "Because he took up here," she said. A few days passed before she was able to get close enough to touch him, and another week for him to lie still in the grass while she pulled ticks off of his ears and backside. He was a nasty old thing and she knew it. He stayed as close to her as he could possibly get at all times, like if he stayed near the one person who liked him no one would make him go back to wherever he came from.

Ethan came down with a bad stomachache one blistering day in August. Abigail stood in his doorway, not saying anything, waiting for him to explain. She looked like she was examining him for leprosy, eyes narrowed, calculating the scene right down to the pack of crackers on the nightstand. "Stomach bug," he said flatly, shivering from a fever.

Abigail turned and left the room. He rolled over and watched out of his bedroom window as she crossed the yard to the line of pine trees on the eastern side of the property. She jumped up and pulled down branches, fiddling with them for a moment and letting them go again. She did this for about five minutes before walking back to the house. He could hear pots and pans being shifted loudly in the cabinet.

Abigail boiled green pine needles and forced him to drink

the water. She called it pine-top tea and said she found the recipe in a book she'd read on the bus. He asked her if it was a fiction book or a real book and she said she didn't know, looking a bit offended. It tasted heinous, and it didn't make him feel any better, but he drank two pots of it anyway. She shelled speckled butter beans on the floor by his bed and wouldn't leave until he drank the last sip.

Ethan had plenty of opportunities to ask her big questions that would help him figure out what the hell she was doing here, but she still wasn't much of a conversationalist. Neither was he, but Ethan felt comfortable enough talking when she was around. While he was sick, he told Abigail about his gaming, about his older brother who gave him this scar and that one, and she sat listening on the floor by his bed, her fingernails green from the beans. The goofy brown dog stayed sprawled out on the rug of his bedroom, happy to be part of the family and out of the heat.

Abigail brought the old TV in from the living room that night, and they flipped through the ten channels, looking for a decent movie. She laughed out loud when Jude Law's character died at the end of *Cold Mountain*. It was the funniest thing she'd ever seen in her life. "He went all that way just to die," she howled, almost spilling the bowl of shelled peas on her lap.

Ethan had not considered what it would feel like to come home and find her gone. She wasn't in the kitchen or the barn when he woke up that morning, and she rarely struck out on her own at this point; she had no need to. He considered calling the cops, but he didn't want to bring the law raining down on her.

Thankfully, the lights were on in the barn the next night when he ended his live stream. He walked the forty paces across the yard and knocked on the door. It gave him a splinter.

For the first time since she showed up, he let himself in.

Abigail was pacing. Ethan wasn't sure he'd ever seen some-one pace outside of movies, but that's sure enough what she was doing, walking from one side of the barn to the other, stepping awkwardly over falling rafters and acting like he wasn't even there. The old radio he'd bought her was on the talk station and he listened for a minute to see if that was stressing her out, but it was something about the correlation between captive carnivore propagation and poaching laws in India.

"Hey, you okay?" he finaly asked.

Abigail stumbled, hitting her toe on a loose floorboard. "Goddamn it."

"Oh fuck, I'm sorry," Ethan said, stepping forward.

She backed away from him like he had a gun, so he froze and lifted his hands a little. Abigail was sweating and wheezing, and her shoulders were shaking.

"Hey," he said, quieter. "What's going on?"

"The dog is gone. He's gone."

"Dogs go missing sometimes. It happens."

"He's my dog."

"He's *a* dog. He probably ran a rabbit into the woods or something. He'll come back."

She murmured something under her breath, but it didn't look like she was listening to herself. He'd never seen her like this. She looked like she was on drugs and her anxiety was hitting him like second-hand smoke, making his heart beat a little too fast for his own comfort. Ethan had only just gotten to a point where he didn't need the anxiety pills Charlie gave him before he left, but Abigail was making him wish he had one now.

"Are you going to send me back?" she asked suddenly.

Ethan furrowed his brow. "No."

"Why?"

"It's not my damn business to send you anywhere. You want to go somewhere, you'll go. You want to stay here, you can stay."

Her eyes were red and swollen. "Then will you look something up for me? On your computer?"

"Yeah, sure," he said, relieved to actually have a course of action. "Come on."

She stumbled a little bit in the dark on the way up the hill. Her knees seemed weak. "I need to know some things about some people," she said when he sat down at his desk.

"You're going to have to be more specific than that."

"They're in Bethany."

Ethan looked at her with a little bit of shock and she averted her gaze like a scared dog.

"You want to know about people in Bethany? Like, news?"

She nodded. He looked back at the screen. It didn't take long for him to find the *Herald's* ancient website on Google, and he hunted along the top of the page for the search bar. She leaned over his shoulder.

"What last name should I type in?" he asked.

"Hatcher. H-A-T—"

"Got it," he said, trying to sound casual for her sake.

That name had a reputation in Bethany—and not a good one. The whole family—a husband, wife, and their two girls—was understood to be white trash in general, especially the dad. Ethan always tried to avoid him if he could, and most people in the town generally felt the same way. His mother had mentioned some nasty drama with them on the phone months ago, but he couldn't remember what it was, something about the older girl going missing. He'd probably been trying to multitask at the time.

Two entries popped up: Sarah Call and Emma Lynn. There were no photos of the two, just a piece of generic clipart by each of their names, the kind they post when there aren't any family members to write something nice, doves with olive branches and lilies. They were obituaries.

He could tell by the birth and death dates that Sarah was in her forties. Emma must have been her daughter—she was eight years old.

Abigail's dark-blue eyes jumped back and forth in the white light of the screen like she wasn't sure what to look at. He hesitated, then used the cursor to draw her attention to the dates of death. "They died a few months back, apparently, not long before I left Bethany. Just a few days apart."

She swallowed something that sounded like it hurt going down. "Can you," she whispered, nodding to the screen. "Can you . . . can I see?"

He clicked on Sarah C. Hatcher's name. She died at the Crawford County Memorial Hospital and had gone to be with the Lord. For the child, Emma Lynn, they offered an even shorter narrative with no details: "She died unexpectedly. In lieu of flowers, donations can be made to the Carolina Association for Suicide Prevention."

Ethan chewed the inside of his cheek for a minute while she digested. "Cousins of yours?" he asked, hopefully. "Or like, distant relatives?"

"Old friends," she said, very slowly standing up straight.

"I'm sorry."

"They're . . . in a better . . ." she began, but stopped, like those light cliché words weighed a ton in her mouth and carrying just one more of them was impossible. Then she stumbled backward. Ethan leapt to his feet to catch her arm, and lowered her into the nearby lawn chair.

He took his hand off of her, but he watched. He felt like she needed someone to watch. She needed someone to witness her chest rising and falling, and to hear the way she was choking on air the way he usually did during his panic attacks. Something loud and explosive was building in her. She was shaking her head and staring at the ceiling, and when she finally blinked, three or four tears fell from each of her eyes at the same time.

Ethan reached behind him to close the page on his computer. Had he known this would happen, he would've tried to do more to protect her from whatever it was she saw. He gave her a few seconds of silence, both of them waiting to see if she could get a hold of herself. When she balled her fists and crushed them against her eye sockets, she let out a guttural moan that answered his unspoken question.

Abigail. Abigail Hatcher.

Ethan wasn't sure what made him spring into action, or how he knew he was supposed to, but he did. He knelt down in front of her chair, resting his hands on her still-knobby knees. "Hey," he said, in a tone he hoped was comforting. "It's all right."

The words were embarrassingly hollow and he knew it, a baby aspirin for a gunshot wound. Abigail groaned again. It was not the groan of a child, or a teenage girl. It was not the groan of someone who got dumped or who lost a band competition or even lost a dog. It was a groan that pierced him. It wounded him. It shook the walls of the tiny house. When she tilted her head forward, spit fell out of her open lips—frozen in a silent scream—and onto her lap.

Looking at her and wondering how Bethany could've been so blind as to ignore whatever it was that was happening in that house, he realized that it might not have been blindness at all. It might've been selective sight. His father left his abandoned business off Third Street, and when it became unsightly, they wanted to turn it into a shiny new fire station. And Ethan remembered the day the Congregational Care Committee asked his mother to not bring Gentry to church, because he was strung out and that made everyone uncomfortable and afraid for their purses. In truth, Gentry's addiction was ugly, and they didn't want to see it. And Gentry's best friend, who was training to be a cop at the peak of his addiction, abandoned Gentry cold turkey so he wouldn't look bad before his graduation. Gentry's problems were ugly, and Dale didn't want to be seen with them.

His mother was the one everyone saw after Gentry died, as guilty as Jackson Hatcher in their eyes. Ethan's father ran. Ethan disappeared into the basement, and she was left to take the blame on her shoulders. All of it. Nettie Coats should've done this. She should've done that. If only she hadn't let him play those violent video games. If only she'd forced him to go to Sunday school. If only she'd sent him to rehab. If only she'd been harder on him about his grades. If only she'd made him do something constructive, like FFA or football. If only she hadn't bought him that pickup truck for his birthday and let him go all over God's green creation for who-knows-why. She should've made him drink chamomile tea. She should've let him stay in jail for a few nights instead of bailing him out that one time.

"Children learn by watching their parents," he had heard a woman whisper after the funeral. Ethan stood with his fists balled up and his eyes lowered to the grass of the Bethany Cemetery. "Makes me wonder about the other one."

The other one, they said.

Abigail tried to clear her throat and dragged the back of her arm over her nose. Ethan stood up to get her some toilet paper.

She was starting to slow down, exhausted. Each breath was a shiver, and her back was perfectly rounded like the mountain.

"Hey," he said, suddenly inspired. "I've got a new game I'm trying out. I'm not even streaming, so you'll be the first to see me play it." Then, he laughed a little. "I'm really bad at first. I have to practice before I go on camera. You can just sit back and watch if you want, if you don't want to be alone."

She was pushing the toilet paper in and out of her nostrils. "That sounds good, yeah," she said, her voice muffled with snot.

He booted up the gaming console and got the blanket from his bed and draped it over her. She nestled down. It was a game about a lone survivor of a zombie apocalypse, a young girl with a backpack and a knife and fast legs.

After an hour, Abigail said, "I don't have anybody." Her voice was hoarse, empty. "I'm alone now."

"No, you're not," he said.

She wanted to go out that night to look for the dog. Ethan gave her a bottle of water and an Oatmeal Creme Pie and tried to tell her that the only thing she'd find in the dark was snakes, but she went anyway. He watched her disappear into the tree line and wondered if she'd ever come back.

Ethan got into his truck next morning to ride the roads. He had no idea what he would do if he actually found the dog. Ethan had never gotten close enough to actually touch it, and he'd never come if Ethan called, but if he could just get eyes on him and tell Abigail with a clear conscience that her mutt was okay, it might give her some peace.

He drove around with the radio on low, scanning the fields and ditches (please, no) until he ran low on gas, which didn't take long. There was a station right by the general store, so he filled up, then walked across the street to get some comfort food for them both. It didn't look like there were a lot of people there, which was just as well. The fewer people that had to hear Ethan's sad attempts at conversation with Kyle, the better.

When he walked in this time, the cowbell banging against the door, Kyle smiled and said, "Hey, Ethan." There was another guy behind the counter on a barstool studying a textbook.

Ethan waved nervously, then found the Little Debbie shelf and scanned it, trying to figure out if there was any way to know what she might want. He decided on Zebra Cakes, Devil Cremes, Pecan Spinwheels, and Nutty Buddies, then knelt down and snatched a handful of Cowtails. When he was in third grade, his father had stopped by the gas station in Bethany every afternoon on the way home from school to buy him a Cowtail and a Pepsi and a bag of peanuts they would split. He hadn't had one since, but he was willing to bet Abigail would like them.

The guy behind the counter said something to Kyle and he laughed. "Stop, dude," he hissed. "You're gonna get me in trouble." Ethan peeked over the top of the aisle to the counter to see Kyle punch him in the arm. "Put your head back in that damn book before I put it there for you."

If they were, and it seemed like they were, how could they be out in public like this? Ethan went to the cooler for a few sodas, now struggling to hold everything in his arms. Kyle finally saw him and jumped up. "Oh, lemme get you a basket."

"Thanks."

"Man, you look like you haven't slept in days."

Ethan dropped his groceries in the basket and took it from him. Looking at all the items from this angle made him look like someone who was very high, or very dumped. "Rough night.

Rough year, actually." *Rough life.* "I'm okay," he said. It was easier to talk to him now for some reason.

"Let me know if I can help you find anything," Kyle said cheerfully.

An older couple walked in, dressed in pastels like they had just come from a wedding. Ethan waited to see if the other guy would straighten up, or slouch farther down, or look a little more manly, or a little less obvious. In fact, Ethan waited for any kind of reaction at all. The man walked over and shook Kyle's hand while Ethan tossed a few packs of gum on top of everything else.

"You boys staying out of trouble?"

You boys?

"You know we never do."

We?

"Y'all better keep your head in those books so you can get into the same school."

Y'all?

"Oh, I'm keeping him straight," Kyle said.

Ethan watched the interaction as well as he could without looking creepy. The older woman was shaking her head but smiling. The man gave Kyle a clap on the shoulder. The other guy nodded and smiled, obviously a bit new to the dynamic, but not nearly as new as Ethan, who had never seen anything like this outside of television shows about New York where everyone did anything they wanted and everyone was okay with it.

"Did you find everything you were looking for?" Kyle asked when Ethan put his basket on the counter and started unloading. The other guy stood up and started bagging the items even though Ethan was fairly certain he didn't actually work here.

"I did," Ethan said, truthfully.

Kyle took his card, swiped it, waited for the machine to spit out a receipt, then said, "Hey, you take care of yourself, man."

Ethan looked up into his eyes for the first time.

"Just, you know, keep your chin up."

"Thank you," Ethan said.

The damn dog was laying on the porch when he got home. Ethan had just finished eating dinner on the porch step when Abigail came out of the woods, looking like a dirty used sponge with all of the water twisted out of it. Her face was pale and sweaty from the heat and a little bit pink with some sunburn. When she saw Tucup sitting with him, she jogged up and then stopped about four feet away from the bottom step. "Oh," she said, sighing. Just that.

Oh.

A quiet two weeks passed. They didn't talk much, but she stayed close to him, and the dog stayed close to her. When she went out to mess around in the garden, Ethan stood on the porch. When he worked, she sat nearby and played Gentry's old games. He was glad to see them being used.

He knew he needed to do something to get them out the rut they were in. So he drove to the general store on a day when he knew Kyle wouldn't be working and bought hot dogs and marshmallows and lighter fluid.

They dug a hole, found some dry logs in the woods, and lit a fire in the yard that night. He bent some metal coat hangers to use as roasting forks and when her first marshmallow caught on fire, she laughed for the first time in weeks.

"How did you make it out this far anyway?" he asked,

gesturing vaguely.

Her eyes blurred and bounced when he looked at them through the air above the fire. "Walked," she finally said, bluntly. "Took a while. People gave me money, so I took the bus when I could. Sometimes cars would stop and give me food or they'd throw it out the window." Abigail sat down on the grass and looked at him. "One lady asked me if I needed a ride. I couldn't tell her where I was going, because I didn't know, so she drove me to a building in the city that had a lot of homeless people in it. I guess that's when I figured out I was homeless. It was nice to have a place to sleep but I wanted to keep going. Something told me I wasn't where I needed to be yet."

Ethan looked at the barn and at the house, then at her. He wondered where Kyle and his boyfriend were, what they were doing that night and what they were doing with their lives. They wanted to go to college. Maybe they were planning to move to New York when they graduated. Maybe Kyle was only staying with his grandparents for the summer and the boyfriend was a temporary thing. Maybe they were engaged . . . it could happen here, now, he knew. Actually, seeing Kyle and his boyfriend made a lot of impossible things seem possible. But whatever they were doing, Ethan knew Kyle would not stay in this town for long. He was too cool, too spirited, too fun to be behind the counter of a general store. He was the kind of guy Ethan admired, the kind of guy who stayed in motion—moving, going.

"I think we need to go back," Ethan said.

"Back?"

"Bethany. I think we need to go back to Bethany."

The embers underneath the wood turned orange against the wind and then faded again. Ashes swept up and floated east. "Why would we do that?" Abigail asked.

"I think the people there need to see you. And they need to see me. And honestly, if we don't go, we'll just be stuck here."

"But if we go back," she said, "We'll be stuck there."

"Well, we need to go back to go forward, I guess. We can't be just a gay dude and an orphan staying in the woods forever. Eventually we're gonna have to do something." Ethan nudged a log deeper into the flames. "We can stay with Mama. You, too. There are two spare bedrooms and a basement that's pretty sweet, if I say so myself." He looked at her, his voice picking up. "There'll be birthdays and Christmases. We'll get you back into school—a different school if you want—and by the time you graduate, you can go to the community college with me or anywhere else you want to go. But we need some roots if we're gonna fly anywhere."

He could tell by looking at her that words like gay and bedroom and college and Christmas and fly were not words that registered with her. That was all the more reason to keep pressing. A marshmallow fell off his stick and puffed up in the fire briefly before it melted. "Look, I'm not going to make you go anywhere. I'm not going to call the cops, and I'm not going to throw you out. But you need to be around people who can help you grow up and function and that's not me." He stabbed a hot dog onto his stick and laughed. "To be honest, it's probably not Mom either, but she'll like having us around."

Abigail swatted at a gnat and stuck another marshmallow on her coat hanger. She spent several long minutes deep in thought. Then she said, "Can the dog come?"

Ethan looked at Tucup, who was laying in the grass a few feet away, hoping for bits of hot dog. "Yeah, we'll all go," he said, figuring that this might be the only way to get her to agree. "We'll all go home."

Ethan was still driving his dead brother's Dodge, and every time he put it on the road, he felt like he was borrowing it. Gentry had kept it in pretty good shape, and after he died, Ethan's mother went out to the shed and started it every few days in the winter. Before he sequestered himself in the basement, he used to watch her do this from his bedroom window. She'd take a beer or a Coke or a cup of something, go out to the shed, lift the door, climb in the truck, start it up, and listen to the radio—sometimes for five minutes, sometimes for an hour, sometimes two or three hours at a time. She never cried. She just sat. She made sure the truck never atrophied like they did.

Everything he and Abigail owned fit in the back of it with room to spare, even the dog. The ride to Bethany only took about an hour and a half. Abigail looked out the window most of the time, watching the white lines shooting by, flying in the opposite direction. They stopped for gas off the highway and Ethan thought about giving her a five and sending her inside for a snack, but her shoulder was plastered to the passenger-side door like she wanted nothing more than to open it and roll out and run away. While the gas was pumping, he sat in the truck and fidgeted with the cheap Wal-Mart cellphone his mother had given him when he left. He considered calling her, but he still felt like he needed to maintain the right to turn around if he wanted to.

There was a new stoplight at the first big intersection in town. They had to sit at it too long for his comfort. People in the cars around them were on their phones or reaching into the backseat or plucking their eyebrows, paying the prodigal children no mind. When they passed the trailer park on the right side, Abigail pressed her nose and both hands against the glass. "There are other people there now," she said quietly. "I'm glad there are other people there now."

Abigail and Ethan went to the cemetery first. It was about the size of two football fields. Most of the graves were flat markers, but a few stuck up from the ground like pillows, and a few more were upright entirely. No one in town had the money for big monuments or even the fancy stone benches that other cemeteries had. Ethan remembered exactly where Gentry's stone was, even though he'd only been there once, at the funeral. He'd seen it many times in his dreams since then.

As they walked, Abigail knelt down and picked up all the plastic flowers that had been blown too far by thunderstorms to know which grave they belonged to. They were worn out and frayed, and she spent much of their trek collecting them into a clumsy, discolored bouquet. Tucup followed her, trotting happily over the graves with his tongue hanging out of his mouth.

His mother had been there, at some point, to switch out the Easter fake flowers for nondescript summer fake flowers, and to rake the storm-strewn leaves off of Gentry's plot. Abigail stood off to the side with her awkward little arrangement, but when she saw there were already flowers in the vase, they drooped by her side.

Ethan punched his hands into his pockets and rocked back and forth, unsure of what to do now that he was here. He had hoped he'd know what to say or pray or think. When Gentry died, he hoped that it would bring their family closer together. He had hoped, when his father left them, that he would take his poisonous grief with him. He had hoped, when he encouraged his mother to date again, that she would find love or at least comfort. He had hoped, when he came out, that it would give him the courage to step outside of his prison. He had hoped, when he tried to burn down his father's auto garage, that he would feel vindicated. He had hoped, when he left town, that he would feel free.

We can be outcasts together, Gentry had told him once.

Ethan looked at Abigail.

"Do you know where they are?" he asked, gesturing to the plastic bouquet.

She shook her head.

"We can look if you want," he said. "We don't have anything better to do."

Abigail shook her head.

"Do you want something to eat, then? We can go to Austin's. It'll be busy, though."

"I remember Austin's," she said, lifting her head and squinting at him in the sun. "They have grilled cheese sandwiches."

On their way out of the cemetery, she took the time to read every marker they passed. Finally, she stopped at Winifred Myron Finnerty, who had died in 1959, and put the flowers in the empty green-copper vase, arranging them meticulously.

"I like her name," she said.

Ethan had hoped the edge of the life he had with his full family would eventually meet the edge of life without them, neatly and symmetrically, but the edges of both were jagged and fucked up and uneven and left giant gaps in his memory, except for one jagged and fucked up and uneven place where his life intersected with Abigail's when it wasn't supposed to, or was. He looked into the gaps around where she was and saw nothing. He was okay with that.

Austin's was bustling with the lunch crowd. Ethan held the door for Abigail when they got there, but she stood back on the sidewalk, waiting for him to lead. So he did. Tucup found a tree and curled up under it. The bells hanging on the door rang out when it closed behind them, and a few people looked up from their coffees and burgers and fries. Abigail visibly moved behind him and stayed there until they got to the counter to place their order.

If Austin himself recognized them, he didn't act like it. Ethan ordered a hot dog and a grilled cheese and fries and two drinks.

Mitchell Canter, Johnny Barnes, Roy Freedman, and Samuel Cotter were sitting at the front table, mouths hidden by their papers and coffee cups. Charlie and her husband, Officer Dale Overton, were sitting in the back corner. They looked pretty content over their burgers and styrofoam cups of sweet tea. Charlie was wearing her ring.

Ethan stared at her. After a few moments, she looked up from her conversation and met his eyes. He had not expected to ever see her again. Some shock registered on her face, enough to make Dale look over his shoulder. He was wearing his police uniform and Abigail flinched, but Dale smiled and waved. Then Charlie did the same.

"Is he going to take me somewhere?" Abigail whispered.

"Doesn't look like it," he said. "I don't think he knows who you are."

"Good."

Dale and Charlie looked at one another, then back down at their food and kept talking about whatever it was married folks talked about. Ethan and Abigail both relaxed. "Charlie knows how to wrangle him. You're safe."

They sat there for an hour, frozen to their seats, re-acclimating to all the movement and chatter and noise. Abigail soaked each fry in a pile of ketchup, her eyes darting back and forth. Some people stared at them when they passed. Some waved sheepishly. Some of them simply smiled and walked out of the door, those Christmas bells announcing their exits at the end of summer.

Ethan listened to the conversations going on around him and realized he couldn't possibly conjure one single opinion about any of them—conversations about recipes, sports, politics, the tobacco festival, child-friendly Halloween costumes, church potlucks, the farmer's market, current wars, past wars. But they all went about their lives. At least there was life for them, here. At least there was life, period.

ACKNOWLEDGMENTS

To Drew Perry, who read my first short story ever—stapled crooked, clumsily written, anxiously placed on his desk—and said, "So it turns out you can write fiction."

To the dozens of people who have put their hands on these pieces over the years via workshops and offered their critiques, kindness, and support for my work.

To the members of my family who have supported me from the beginning.

To Alaina, Bryan, Gio, James, Jenna, Jillian, Kristin, Kyle, Lydia, Mary, Miya, Rusty, Sunny, and Vincent, who all kept me sane during those years when the blinking cursor was attempting to make me less so, and to Jackie, Titus, Tom, and Will, who read the absolute worst of my pitiful childhood attempts at storytelling and continued being my friends anyway.

To my agent, Lauren Scovel and the Laura Gross Literary Agency, who never stopped believing in this book—and, more remarkably, in me.

To the English Department at Elon University, the University of North Carolina at Wilmington's Creative Writing

Department, and the North Carolina State University's Department of English, whose halls I will always feel honored to have walked.

To Wilton Barnhardt, Belle Boggs, Mark Cox, Nina de Gramont, John Kessel, Cassie Kircher, Rebecca Lee, Jill McCorkle, Tita Ramirez, and Rebecca Pope-Ruark, who taught me to face my fear of the desk and trust my instincts while digging through all the things that horrified me in the search for some tiny fleck of Truth.

To J.T. who lives in the world I tried to depict here, and helped me get it right.

To Taylor, who has taught me so much about what true friendship can be.

To Mandy, who has taught me so much about what true mentorship can be.

To Mamaw, who taught me so much about what true kindness can be.

To Kevin, who has taught me so much about what true love can be.

To my Mama Bear, who taught me so much about who I could be.

And of course, to Sherlock, because writing a book without a good dog laying nearby almost isn't worth doing.